D-CITY UNDERWORLD

Zontae's Reign
3

A NOVEL BY

ANNITIA L. JACKSON

ACKNOWLEDGMENTS

I just want to take this time to say thanks to my husband, Ron Jackson, for encouraging me and having my back while I took a step out on faith. Thank you for being an amazing father to our son, Nathan, and keeping his five-year-old energy at bay while I write. You are my soulmate and helped me to understand what real love is. Thank you for being understanding when I have to write, and you say, "Baby, I got this. You just go do what you need to do." I love you and Nathan to the moon and beyond.

I want to also thank my middle school teacher, Barbara Middlebrooks, for introducing me to writing. You woke up a fire in me that I never knew existed.

To my personal reading crew, Zeanola, Undrea, Shawauna, Diedra, Kimessia, Aundrea, Stacey, Michelle, Sharene, HuAnna, Brittany, Kristi and Marcia that will share their opinions both good and bad, I want to thank you for helping me. I love you ladies so much!!

I would also like to thank my sister, Kasandra, my cousin, Ingrid, and my nephew, Robert. Also, I would like to thank my aunt Gale for her spiritual guidance. You guys are my inspiration for going after my dream of being an author. I have watched you all accomplish your goals, and it inspired me. And to my riders who always have my back, Renee and Freda, I love you both so much.

I also want to thank the ladies in Bookies for taking a chance on my book and helping get the word out about it! Love you, admins!!!

Zee, I have so much love and respect for you and all you do. You are amazing, and you have been a true blessing to me. I always tell people how much you mean to me and the other authors you help. Continue to do your thing because you are a true queen.

My Law! I love you to death because you always give me honest and real conversation. You are one of the first people I see in my inbox in the morning, and I know that my mood, if bad, will be lifted. Thank you for helping me with my book and making my details one hundred. Thank you also for reading my work and keeping me laughing.

LIT-erary Plugs!! You ladies are the real MVP's! You ladies are very important to me. I value your opinions and comments because they have really helped me grow as an author. Each one of you have helped me, and I can't thank you enough.

Thank you to my amazing editor and her crew that keep my work tight. I love you all so much.

I would like to thank God for blessing me with the opportunity to do something that I love to do. Because without Him, I wouldn't be here today or have the storytelling gift that He blessed me with.

SYNOPSIS

When we left the Duvall clan, they were dodging bullets. That is nothing compared to what they will face in the upcoming battle against Queen Esha and Luke. The Underworld has been turned upside down. Friends are turning into enemies, and more devastating truths are being revealed.

Which child has been cursed with the Forbidden Book? Who is the mystery man that came with Dana? Who will live, and who will die in the quest for the crown? Find out in the shocking conclusion to D-City Underworld: Zontae's Reign.

PREVIOUSLY FROM UNDERWORLD
2...

The Council Meeting- Zontae

*M*onster, Draven, Kaidan, Angel, and Dantez were sitting at a table set up specifically for these meetings. We all sat on the left side, while my mother and her minions sat on the right.

"Alright. We are here to determine who the rightful heir to the Underworld is. Queen Esha challenges that she is the rightful heir due to questionable circumstances by her son Zontae, who was named the heir by King Zaire before he passed. The Most High, rest his soul. Also, we need to determine if Queen Esha deserves the plea for asylum. We will allow Queen Esha to speak on why she feels she needs asylum and why she should be named queen. Queen Esha, you have the floor," Kaidan said.

Esha stood up and strolled to the front of the room and began to spin her web of lies, trying to get an Academy Award for her performance.

"First of all, let me say thank you for allowing me to speak, because I have a lot to say. First and foremost, my son is not capable of running the Underworld. Ever since his father has been deceased, things have fallen apart. Even before his father died, it was I who was ruling because his father was an abusive blood whore! I struggled throughout our bond to stay alive. Now, I love my son, but unfortunately, he is much like his father—inadequate to rule. Countless Underworlders have become addicted to the B-Packs that my son has mixed up.

Then he goes against the laws that were put in place by our council and mates with a woman who knows nothing about our ways. He abandoned Jade, one of our own, because of her. We know nothing about this new mate of his and what her powers might mean to the Underworld; she could be very dangerous. Zontae is unstable due to the incubus blood running through him. What's to stop him from going crazy and killing human women, exposing us all? You know that I am more than capable of ruling the Underworld; I will protect it with my life. Zontae and Mesa are my sons but have been corrupted by those two women. I wouldn't be surprised if my sons didn't kill my husband themselves just to rule. The Underworld needs stability; it needs me," Esha stated as she walked back to her chair.

My eyes instantly turned red when she said we killed our father. I was trying to calm down, but the demon in me was raging, and I growled.

Kaidan cleared his throat and said, "The first order of business is asylum. If granted, she has asked that a spell be cast to ensure her safety. The person that kills her will instantly die as soon as her heart stops."

"Hell naw! That gives her the right to do whatever the fuck she wants because no one wants to die behind her ass! This is some bullshit, and you know it! She killed your fucking king, and nobody is going to hold her ass responsible for it? Fuck that! Don't give her asylum so I can avenge my father's death!" Mesa yelled.

Selene pulled him back down in the chair and started rubbing his back to calm him down.

Kaidan shook his head and replied, "Prince Mesa, believe me, I understand how you feel. Even though I have heard the rumors along with everyone else in the Underworld, we can't put her on trial for the murder of King Zaire because we don't have proof that she did it. If you ever find that proof, believe me, she would be on trial for her crimes. We have to abide by the rules, and you know that. Now please refrain from yelling out until after the decisions have been made."

Mesa nodded his head reluctantly and stared down Esha, who was wearing a smile.

Kaidan stood up and said, "We have heard what Queen Esha had to say. We will open the floor if anyone has anything to say about the petition for asylum or the claim to the throne."

The door burst open, and the Harper brothers strolled in. Mesa and I stood in front of our mates with our fangs lengthened and eyes glowing in case they were on some shit. We knew they were coming, but we also knew how shady their family was.

Devin stopped in front of us, and Dane walked over to Luke and punched him in the face. Before they could start fighting, two of the council members broke them up.

"I hate your ass! I am going to kill your ass as soon as I get to you!" Dane yelled as he was being dragged away from Luke.

"Everyone, settle down. Dane, why are you interrupting our council meeting? If you have something to say, say it!" Kaidan yelled.

Dane's eyes glowed blue as he stared at his father with hate.

"The council should know that my father used the Forbidden Book and turned it into a being. We have been tracking everywhere trying to find out where it could be. We finally traced it back to here; the Forbidden Being has been here all along. His sick ass put it in a damn baby! The baby was born this morning!" Dane yelled.

We all stood there in shock at the announcement. A feeling of dread came over me thinking about the implications. Our babies were born this morning. Could one of them be the Forbidden Being? What the fuck did that mean if they were?

"You bastard! How could you do something like that! I promise you I had no clue he was dabbling in the dark arts; he fooled me too!" Esha yelled.

"I call bullshit!" said a raspy female voice I had never heard before.

Esha gasped, and Luke turned white as a ghost.

My uncle stared at her with glowing red eyes.

We all turned to see a woman standing there with curly short hair and glowing eyes, one blue and one green. Beside her was a dark-skinned, tall, muscular man that was at least six eight. In his arms was a body wrapped in a blanket.

Nichelle whispered, staring in shock, "It can't be..."

"Who are you? State your business!" Kaidan yelled.

"My name is Dana Harper, the Watcher and wife to Luke Harper and mother to his four children. I am here to testify against my husband and Queen Esha! They have committed murders, treason, kidnapping, and adultery," Dana answered.

Kaidan replied, "Do you have proof to your allegations?"

Dana smiled and replied, "Yes, I was there when she killed Queen Nichelle's husband, Mason Cantrell. I have two other witnesses to her crimes; the man in the blanket is her husband, Santonio, who Queen Esha and Luke have been holding for years. The man holding him was supposed to die many years ago. His name is M—"

POP! POP! POP!

Bullets started flying everywhere in the room, and bodies started dropping. I pushed Samara down to the floor as I felt two bullets hit me in my back. I knew it was silver because I instantly started getting nauseous and the pain was increasing.

I kept hearing screams, gunshots, and glass breaking as I tried to hang on. That eerie feeling I had earlier was right. All hell had broken loose!

The Hospital-Ever & Zoom (From Loving a Heartless Queen)

I woke up with my body feeling very strange. The lights were brighter, the sounds were louder, and I was very hungry. I opened my eyes, and Zoom was sitting on one side of me, and Dr. Phillips was sitting on the other side. I could tell I was in one of the rooms at the hospital, which was strange to me. Why wasn't I in a regular hospital?

"Hey, beauty. I know you have a lot of questions, and believe me, you will get your answers very soon. How do you feel?" Zoom asked.

I thought about the shape that I was in before and realized that I wasn't in pain and nothing felt broken.

"I feel good, which couldn't be right. I had a lot of broken bones, and I was near death. You two aren't human, are you?" I asked.

They looked at each other and then at me and shook their heads 'no.' I wasn't quite ready for the answer to what they were, because that would mean asking what I was. I knew I was supposed to be dead, and I wasn't. Not to mention, there were no injuries to me at all. But I did have a question for Dr. Phillips that had been plaguing me.

"Why did you help me, Dr. Phillips?" I asked.

"I am your uncle. Your father was my brother. I never knew who your mother was, because he was killed before he could tell me. I lost contact with you two until I found you in college," Dr. Phillips answered.

I sat in the bed in shock and thought about all that he had done for me in the past few years, and now I knew why.

"I think I should give you two a minute. Let me go grab you something to drink," Zoom said.

He left out, and my uncle continued his story without asking.

"I would have taken you girls in if I hadn't been given a mission that was of the utmost importance. A long time ago, I was asked to protect someone that was in danger and needed protection. Hold on; he has been waiting to see you," my uncle said.

When he opened the door, it was John Doe, and he had some pictures in his hands.

"It's good to see you, Dr. Moore. I am glad that you are okay. My memory has come back to me recently, and you are the reason why. It seems that your therapy has helped me out a great deal. Someone put a spell on me to make me forget who I am. But unfortunately for some, I remember it all. Here are the pictures of my family," John Doe stated.

I looked at the first two photos and was about to grab the other one from him and look, when Zoom walked in and dropped the drinks he had in his hand, spilling them all over the floor. He immediately kneeled in front of John Doe. I found that strange as hell, but my life was now nothing but strange events.

"Zoom, why are you kneeling in front of my patient?" I asked.

"He is supposed to be dead, but this is our King Zaire Duvall," Zoom answered.

I was still confused because of the whole king situation and him coming back from the dead. I was about to ask some questions, when I noticed the picture in his hand. My eyes grew large, and I felt like the wind had been knocked out of my lungs.

"Umm, excuse me, King Zaire, why do you have a picture of my mother?" I asked.

Everyone looked at me with shock as I grabbed and held up the picture.

Zoom was the first to speak.

"What the fuck! Esha is your mama?"

PART I

"The Forbidden Book"

"Things have got to get better. Just remember that there can't be sunshine without rain. We have been going through some storms! So, we should be having some sunny weeks coming soon

— SAMARA

PROLOGUE-25 YEARS AGO

KING ZAIRE

I was walking through the estate, looking for my wife Esha. I loved my wife, don't get me wrong, but my heart would always belong to Nichelle, even though she loved another man. I loved her enough to let her go and be happy, if that was what she wanted.

I had moved on with Esha only because I wanted sons and she was willing to give me what I wanted. I now had two handsome young men, who I loved with all my heart. They would both run the kingdom the way it should be run. The watcher had seen it in a vision. Zontae would be king, and Mesa would be his right hand as prince. I would love to have a daughter to complete my legacy, but my wife was tripping about giving me what I wanted.

That was one of the reasons I was looking for her now. My dick was hard, and I wanted to drop some seeds inside my wife to see if we could make this little girl that I wanted so badly. Hell, I was worried that she would end up with Esha's attitude, but hopefully, she would be just like my boys.

I walked around the corner and heard moaning. It sounded like someone was fucking, but nobody would disrespect my house like that.

I turned the corner, and I was shocked to see my wife being fucked in the ass by Luke and was riding a shifter who was in wolf form. Then she was sucking Dantez's dick! This bitch was getting fucked all kinds of ways, and it made me sick to my stomach! My eyes were glowing green, and my fangs and claws dropped because I was getting ready to kill them all.

Before I could get to them, Dana pulled me back.

"You can't kill them, Zaire. You would be killing half the council, and your boys would be the ones to suffer. You know that they would kill them and not blink twice," Dana stated.

She was right. The penalty for killing the council was steep. But the rage inside of me was boiling over. I didn't love her, but I thought we had a mutual respect. I wanted her dead!

"King Zaire, I have foreseen your death at Esha's hands, and I think you need to leave," Dana replied.

I looked at her like she had lost her mind and responded, "I am not leaving my boys with her! It's no telling what she will do to them if I am not around."

Dana smiled and said, "Who said you won't be around? Stone is a Morph and can change into anyone and mimic them. Morphs are not immortal; they only live two hundred years, and Stone is coming up on his time to pass. He would be honored to take your place and die with honor, protecting his king. You could go into hiding and wait until Zontae is crowned king to come back and kill Esha and the members on the council that are against you. Most of those council members would have retired, and their children would have taken over."

I liked that plan. I could kill Esha, Luke, and Dantez for their betrayal and get away with it. I wasn't sure who the shifter was she was fucking, but it wouldn't be too hard to find out. I just hated leaving my boys.

"I know it will be hard leaving your boys, but it is for the best. If you stay, you will derail their true destiny, and they are destined for greatness. You leaving will help them to achieve it. I have an elixir that can make you forget for a while, and I have a place that you can hide where you will be safe, and no one will think to look for you there. I have a connection there that will help us. Esha has destroyed his family too, so he will be more than happy to help," Dana explained.

I agreed with her because it was what was best for my boys. I spoke with Stone and let him know some key facts to help him in his mission. I said goodbye to my sons, even though they had no clue that is what I was doing. I avoided Esha at all cost, for fear I would choke her hoeish ass and leave her rotting in the cemetery. Once I got settled into the hospital that would be my home for the next twenty years, I took the elixir, and slowly, my memories started to fade.

SAMARA (MARA)

*E*verything just seemed to explode once Dana made her announcement. The bullets started flying, and I was thrown to the floor. I was tired of this shit. I watched my husband wince in pain and realized he had been hit by the bullets that were flying. Fuck this!

I eased out from under him when he wasn't looking. I rose up and concentrated my powers on the earth outside. The ground started to shake a little inside, but a lot outside, and the gunfire stopped outside, as people started screaming, "Earthquake!" Slice and members of the Dynasty Boyz drew their weapons and headed outside and started firing at whoever was out there.

Since that was taken care of, I looked down at my husband and felt the silver elements in his body. I raised my hand and called the silver to me, pulling it straight out so it wouldn't damage anything coming out. I felt the sweat on my forehead, letting me know that I was still getting used to controlling two things at once. I finally saw them on the edge of the wounds and called them the rest of the way out and fell to the floor.

The wounds on his back healed instantly, and he came over to me.

"You are hardheaded as hell! You know you need to get used to using your powers on multiple things. Here, your nose is bleeding. I have to check on everyone else. I need to see who was firing on us too. Stay down until it's all clear," Zontae stated, pressing his bandana to my nose.

Selene scooted over to me and helped me put pressure to my nose.

Zontae and Mesa ran outside.

"We have to find Mom; help me up," I stated.

Selene helped me up, and we started looking for our mom, Dana, and our father. I was a little disoriented from using my magic, but I had to figure out what the hell was going on.

"Can you believe that shit that just went down? I mean, Dana came in spilling all the tea," Lene joked.

I laughed because the look on Esha's face was priceless.

We got to the back of the room where a lot of people were standing. Nichelle was standing there with Dana, Santonio, and the other man that was with her. Dana was in a chair, and everyone was around her.

"Mama, are you okay? Did everyone make it through the shooting alright?" I asked.

Nichelle nodded her head 'no' with tears in her eyes, and replied, "No. Dana was hit four times in the chest. The silver is slowly killing her. We need a healer fast, but I am not sure one will make it here in time."

I looked at Selene, and she nodded her head 'yes.' She always knew what I was thinking. We were a team.

"Watch out for Zontae. The last thing I need is for him to see that I am pushing myself too far," I whispered to Lene.

"Put her on the floor. Make sure to put something under her head and keep her still," I told my mama.

Nichelle did as I asked but looked at me strangely.

"What are you doing, Mara?" Nichelle asked.

"I am calling to the elements in the bullets. They are silver, so I can feel them just like any other element. I just need to concentrate and get them to move straight out without causing any damage. Looking at her chest; one is close to her heart, so I need you to keep her very still, and no one disturb me while I am working on her," I explained.

I looked over at my father, Santonio, as he stared at me. He had a small smile on his face, and I wondered if he recognized me. We looked a lot alike, and it was strange to see him in the flesh.

I nodded my head to him and then looked back down at Dana, to concentrate on healing her. My head still hurt from causing the earthquake outside and getting the bullets out of Zontae, but this woman was instrumental in helping my family stay alive. I would do anything I could to help save her life.

I called upon the Most High to help me in my task. Then I concentrated on the three bullets that would be easier to get out. I spread my hands over the holes and called to the silver, bringing it out slowly in a straight path so that it wouldn't damage anything else. When the bullets appeared at the opening of the wounds, Selene pulled them out.

"Are you okay?" Santonio asked.

I felt my face and nose bleeding, and I was sure that I looked like shit, but I wasn't stopping until I got the final bullet out. Then she could heal on her own.

"I'm fine; just an occupational hazard," I replied.

Nichelle was looking at me with worried eyes, and she was studying me. I needed to hurry up before she stopped me.

I placed both my hands over the final wound close to her heart. I closed my eyes and pictured the bullet coming out in a straight line away from her heart. I called the silver slower than I did the first three bullets. I moved it inch by inch away from her beating heart. I felt sweat pouring down my face, and I tasted blood from my nose bleeding. I was fading fast, but I refused to let her die. I called the silver a little more once it got past the main part of the heart. I felt it gliding by it, and it pushed up to the hole in the wound where Selene pulled it out.

I heard everyone take a breath, but I didn't want to open my eyes. I was too tired. I felt myself wobble and knew I was falling. I felt someone catch me and scoop me up. It wasn't my husband—I knew his feel—so I pried my eyes open and looked into the light brown eyes of the stranger that Dana brought with her.

"I gotcha, sis. My name is Monroe, by the way, but everyone calls me Mon for short," he stated.

He used the bandana that I had wrapped around my hand to wipe the blood from my nose. I looked at him, and there was a calmness to his face, but for some reason, I sensed he was more like a volcano, waiting to erupt.

I heard a growl and knew who it was instantly.

"Get your fucking hands off my mate before I kill you dead where you stand." Zontae continued to growl.

Monroe laughed, and I didn't like where this was going. Zontae's eyes were pure red and Monroe's turned into pure black, which was strange to me. What was Monroe?

Nichelle stepped in between the two and turned to Zontae.

"Zontae, he is not trying to put claims on your mate. That is Monroe, Mara's brother. She used too much of her powers healing Dana, and she collapsed. He caught her and was tending to her. That's all," Nichelle explained.

Those angry red eyes moved from Monroe to me. Aww fuck! I clenched on to Monroe tighter. It was an involuntary move that I didn't even know I was doing.

"You are scaring my sister, so I think you need to turn it down a notch. I am not releasing her until you calm the fuck down," Monroe stated.

"Who the fuck you talking to like that, bruh? That's your king and more importantly that's my brother, and I will go to war with your ass over him, so bring it, big black ass Popeye looking motherfucker!" Mesa yelled.

This was getting out of hand, and I knew that I would have to face my husband eventually, so I tried to get out of Monroe's arms and got dizzy and fell right back into them. Now the red had gone from my husband's eyes, and there was a look of concern in the green ones that were now looking back at me.

"Baby, you know you are new to using your powers. You have no clue of the damage you caused outside. Not to mention healing me and Dana. I think you need to see what your powers can do and why you don't need to overuse them, or you could end up killing yourself," Zontae stated.

Zontae motioned for Monroe to bring me outside. Monroe followed with him and Mesa side-eyeing each other. I just shook my head. Mesa really didn't like many people.

When we got outside, my mouth opened in shock. The ground everywhere was split open and some cars had fallen into the cracks. Trees had fallen everywhere, and some of the houses had damage.

"Oh no! Did I kill any innocent people?" I asked with tears in my eyes.

"No, baby. The damage is primarily around the estate, which we own, and most of the homes are empty because Esha made them leave. Now, some of the people shooting at us weren't so lucky," Zontae stated.

"Who was shooting at us?" I asked.

Zontae and Mesa exchanged looks, and for some reason, I knew it was bad.

"It was the hunters. With everything that Esha has been doing, she attracted too much attention. Now the hunters have the Underworld in their sights," Zontae said.

"I have no clue how we are going to get them off our backs either," Mesa added.

"So, it's probably going to get worse since I killed some of their people, right? I asked.

"I have a connection with the hunters; let me talk to them," Monroe responded.

"Yo, how do you have a connection to them? Most supernatural creatures stay far away from them," Mesa said, eyeing Monroe suspiciously.

"I'm different. Just remember that when you think about trying me; it will save you a lot of time and energy," Monroe stated.

Monroe walked over to Zontae and transferred me over to his arms.

"My sister needs to feed to feel better. I am trusting that you will take care of her. That goes for you and your brother. I have gone decades without my family; to know that I have two sisters means the world to me. As you said earlier, Mesa, I will go to war over them, so you better treat them with the respect they deserve. Now let me go and see about cleaning up this mess with the hunters," Monroe replied and placed a kiss on my forehead.

After he stepped away to use his phone, Zontae bit his wrist and placed it in my mouth. I drank deeply, but not enough to weaken him. I used my tongue to seal the wound and told my kitty to calm down. The succubus demon wanted to be fed too, but her ass would have to wait because too much turmoil was going on right now.

"Your brother is going to make me beat his ass! Shit, what the fuck is he anyway? I can't tell by his scent or his eyes. If it's anything like that shit y'all got going on, I might have to hit his ass over the head first and then whoop his ass while he's out cold!" Mesa said.

I shook my head because Mesa was crazy, and replied, "You better leave my brother alone. Hell, I don't know what he is, but I sense a lot of power from him. Plus, Lene might beat that ass if you mess with her brother, or not give that ass up!"

Mesa stood there for a moment in deep thought.

"On second thought, we need to welcome our new brother in with open arms, especially in these times of need," Mesa replied.

I shook my head and asked Zontae to put me down. The feeding helped, and I was ready to get back in and see what was going on.

We walked back in, and a few of the council members were talking to Dana while Dane and Devin watched. There were a few missing, and I wondered where they went to. Nichelle and Santonio were talking to each other, and it made me wonder what they were saying.

Then I looked around and got seriously pissed the fuck off. I didn't see Esha, Luke, Jade, or Jazz anywhere. Where had their asses disappeared to? Why did I get a bad feeling that I wouldn't like the answer to that question?

LUKE

"*I* can't believe that your stupid ass wife showed up and ruined my chances of being queen! I had it in the bag and would have gotten the votes that I needed! Not to mention that you didn't tell me that you put the damn Forbidden Book in a baby! Even I wouldn't do anything like that! The whole Underworld will be after our heads over that shit!" Esha yelled.

I didn't see what her ass was yelling about. Once I possessed the Forbidden Book magic, I would be unstoppable. Hell, I was going to give her ass some, but the way she was acting had me rethinking some things.

I looked around, and Jazz, Jade, Cas, Vice, Dantez, and Angel were all here with us. I guess I knew where the votes were coming from on the council. Them motherfuckers were pussy whipped when it came to Esha.

"Look, I had to do what I had to do when it came time to put the being in someone. My first thought was a baby because then I could easily take the powers away from them. As far as Dana showing up, that's your fucking fault! I wanted to kill the bitch a long time ago, but you said 'no, killing a watcher is bad luck.' Well, guess what? Keeping one alive is bad luck too. Now what we need to do is track down this baby. I already can sense their presence. I just have to follow the trail," I explained.

Esha looked at me like I had lost my mind and replied, "I am not going to be wasting my time searching for some baby. Now that the Underworld knows my secrets, I must build an army because Nichelle and her brats, along with my sons, are coming for me! I need to see how my experiment is going on the humans, and I have Samara's blood. I need to see if I can make a serum that I can use to gain some of her powers. Don't you think that all of that is more important!"

I saw we had two different agendas, and I was not giving up my mission for hers. I had been doing that for decades, and it was my turn to have all the power in the Underworld.

"Esha, I am leaving to find the child, and that's all I have to say on the matter. I can meet up with you later, but I have a destiny to fulfill, and getting those powers are my number one priority, so I guess we part ways for now. It looks like you have enough dick to keep you company anyway," I stated.

Dantez laughed, and Angel didn't say anything.

"Esha, I told you a long time ago that we had your back. Now that we have split from the council, we can rain havoc down on the different realms and create a war between the different kingdoms. That would buy you some time to get more people on your side. Since I am King of the Seraphim realm, you have my people backing you in a war. Then you have Angel who is King of the Spirit realm; that is enough to start some mischief and get some things started. Our warriors will protect you. You don't need Luke," Dantez stated.

Esha smiled and leaned into him. I was done. She could fuck whomever she wanted. Once I had the power, she would be forced to bow down to me.

"Fine. We part ways here. I wish you well, Esha, and I hope that you get all that you desire. Jazz and Jade, come on," I commanded.

Jazz followed beside me, but Jade stopped.

"I'm sorry, Daddy, but I am going with Esha," Jade said.

I looked at her for a moment and realized she had always been with Esha, so it was better I left her where she was.

19

"Cas, are you coming?" I asked

Cas shook her head 'no.' "Sorry, Unc. I am going where the money is, and right now, she has the warehouse with the B-Packs in them. Unc, I am sending Vice with you to watch your back. You are still my family, and I want you to know that I am not choosing this bitch over you; it's all about the money. Hit me up if you need me."

Esha looked offended and replied, "I am a queen, and you need to address me as such."

Cas laughed and replied, "Well excuse me. I am going with the queen of the bitches to get my shit from the warehouse so I can get on my hustle."

I wasn't sticking around to hear what else they had to say. I had to find this baby and quickly. We flashed over to an open field where I stood and pulled my knife out of my pocket and sliced my hand and smeared the blood on my forehead. I closed my eyes and whispered the Forbidden Book's true name into the wind and waited for it to respond. A vision hit me, telling me the exact place where I could find the Forbidden Book. I was shocked at first, but then a smile spread across my face. The time for power and revenge was at hand.

SYREN

J was downstairs fixing the bottles of breast milk that Selene and Samara had left for Zaire, Zaniyah, and Mena. Their little asses were thick as thieves and would cry their cute butts off if you put them in separate cribs, so they were all sleeping in one. I loved taking care of them because I couldn't have children, so this was my way of having that experience, but the sad part was I had to give them back at the end.

Omega came in, and he never said much to me unless he was breaking up a fight between his brother and me. Alpha worked my last nerve! He was just like my last boyfriend that left me lying bloody and broken, unable to have kids and with a broken heart.

"I'm sorry about my brother. He usually only deals with women of loose morals, so you are a challenge to him. I am glad that you speak your mind and set him straight though. He needs that in his life. You are more than meets the eye, Ms. Syren. I love it; beauty and spirit," Omega stated.

I smiled and replied, "Well, your brother needs to get some manners because he is rude as hell and needs to learn how to speak to people. Especially women."

Omega started helping me clean up, and we both grabbed the dish towel at the same time. I felt chills run down my spine at the contact, and I pulled back.

Omega stared into my eyes, and I felt something I hadn't felt in a long time: attraction.

"I'm not interrupting anything, am I?" Alpha said, staring at the both of us.

Omega shook his head and smiled. "Naw, bruh. We were just cleaning up the kitchen. I will head out and check to make sure no one has breached the ring of protection that Nichelle put up. Nice talking to you, Syren."

Omega walked out of the kitchen, and I started to get the bottles out of the bottle warmers. Alpha spun me around and got in my face.

"So you like my brother, huh? The boring, quiet kind that don't challenge you and make your body burn up the way that I do. You took my dick, so you already know I can more than satisfy all your desires, princess. Don't fear the monster. I'm sure you can find ways to tame him," Alpha said with a smile.

He rubbed my arms, and I felt the same chills, but this time I felt a feeling of lust. The same feelings that started me down my road of trouble before. Not to mention, I shouldn't be having feelings for two brothers.

I moved past Alpha, gathering the bottles so that I could take them up for the babies' feedings. It was almost time for them to wake up. I started up the steps, and I could have sworn I heard voices. One of them sounded familiar.

I eased back down the steps and ran into Alpha's chest.

"Go get Omega. I hear them too. Call my cousin; I will go and see what's up," Alpha whispered.

I flashed to Omega and grabbed him, flashing him with me to the house.

"Someone's here; Alpha went to check, but I am going up there. The babies are my responsibility," I whispered.

He nodded his head without missing a beat and pushed me behind him as he headed for the steps. As we got to the steps, we heard fighting going on.

We ran into the room, and the first thing I noticed was Jazz holding Mena up by her leg. My eyes instantly went white with rage. I raised my hand and flashed Mena over to me and gave her a quick once over to make sure she was okay. I used my powers to send her into the bassinet in Nichelle's room. There was an extra spell protecting her door.

When I turned around, I was sliced in the face by Jazz's claws. I backhanded her into the wall, and she slid down it. I looked over at Alpha, and he was fighting to get through a shield around Luke who had Zaniyah in his arms, looking at her in a strange way. Omega was fighting with a man, but I couldn't see who because he was blocking him.

I sent a bolt of energy into the shield to try and punch a hole into the surface. I was a sorceress, but I was still in training and no match for Luke. But I would die before I let him hurt those babies.

I felt a slice across my ankle which made me lose focus on Luke's shield. This bitch was really getting on my nerves!

"Leave my daddy alone, bitch!" Jazz yelled.

I didn't want to waste any magic because I would need all of it for Luke's shield. So, I grabbed Jazz by her hair and started punching her in the face. When she tried to get up, I kneed her in the stomach. I grabbed her clawed hand and twisted it, ramming the sharp claws into her own neck. She started gurgling on her own blood and collapsed. That should keep her out for a while, regenerating.

I turned my gaze on Luke's shield and tried to use as much power as I could to break through.

Alpha came over and said, "You got to hurry up! He is sucking the breath out of Zaire, and it's some weird black stuff coming out of him. I'm going to help my brother so we can all beat the shit out of Luke!"

Oh no! The only thing that this could mean was that there was black magic in baby Zaire! I didn't give a damn what he had in him; Luke had to stop, or he would kill him!

"Luke! Stop! He is a baby, and if you keep it up, you could kill him!" I yelled while still applying pressure.

His voice pounded into my head and replied, "Fuck you and this little bastard! I plan to suck the life out of him just to make the Duvalls suffer. Try if you want to, little witch, to stop me, and I promise that you will die along with him!"

"Die it is then!" I replied and intensified my magic into his shield. Zaniyah was screaming, and baby Zaire was too quiet for my liking. The shield was getting thinner, so I yelled for Alpha to try breaking through it as I kept up the assault on it. Alpha was able to punch through it and hit Luke in the face, which caused him to drop baby Zaire. I used my powers to send both babies into Nichelle's room. I was terrified about how baby Zaire was.

Luke sent a blast to Alpha's chest, sending him crashing into the walls, knocking a hole in it. I sent a blast into Luke's side, putting a hole in his side. He turned his gaze on me, and I prepared for the blast until I was tackled. I looked into the eyes of my former boyfriend, Vice.

"Stay down and pretend to be dead," he whispered in my ear and placed a kiss on my neck.

I lay still as I heard Omega and Alpha battling Luke. Vice placed another kiss on the side of my neck and got up, picking up an unconscious Jazz in his arms.

"Come on, Luke! We have to get out of here! Your daughter is injured, and reinforcements could be coming at any moment! You got what you came for!" Vice yelled and flashed away.

Luke's face was messed up from the battle between him and the brothers. While he was busy trying to get away, I flashed to Nichelle's room and said the words that would let me in.

Zaniyah and Mena were screaming at the top of their lungs, but baby Zaire wasn't moving. I screamed, thinking that I failed him and his parents. I saw a faint amount of black smoke floating around his mouth. That meant that some of it was still in his system, and he was still breathing.

I checked his pulse, and it was very faint. I scanned him, and CPR wouldn't help. Part of his life force had been drained from him. I was feeling woozy and looked down, and blood was pouring from the gashes in my leg that Jazz had made. I didn't know they were that deep. It came to me in an instant on what I needed to do to save baby Zaire.

I wrote a message down on the paper that was beside the bed. I calmed Zaniyah and Mena down and kissed them on their heads. I grabbed baby Zaire and laid him on my chest. I said an incantation that was forbidden unless in dire circumstances. I felt the magic being taken from my core and watched it float into baby Zaire's mouth. I smiled as his chest started to rise more and his eyes popped open and were hazel now instead of the black color he was born with. I felt drained and knew my powers were gone. With them being gone, I couldn't heal the wound on my leg. I watched as baby Zaire cooed and put his fist in his mouth.

My leg burned, and I could feel my life slip away. But literally trading my life for his was well worth the sacrifice.

OMEGA

After Syren got away, Alpha and I started attacking Luke, trying to kill his ass for hurting the babies and Syren. My fangs dropped, and my claws extended. My wings sprouted from my back, and I flew at him and sliced his chest open.

Alpha's Incubus characteristics came out too, and we started slicing pieces off Luke's body. Blood was everywhere, and I knew his ass was about to die soon.

But then something strange happened; Luke's eyes changed to the oddest midnight blue color and then started glowing. I had never seen that color in an Underworlder. I felt a sharp pain in my chest and fell to the ground. It felt like my heart was being ripped out. I looked over at Alpha, and he was writhing in pain as well.

Luke was smiling the evilest smile, and his face and body were turning jet black, and his muscles were getting bigger. He raised his hands above us like he was about to deliver a killing blow, but bluish blood started pouring from his nose and eyes. He reached up to wipe his eyes and stared in shock at the blue blood on his fingers. Luke screamed and flashed out of the house.

The pain in my chest had eased, and I stood up as my claws, wings, and fangs receded. I walked over to Alpha and helped him up.

"What the fuck was that! Did you see his ass turn black and start bleeding blue? I don't know what the hell is going on, but we need to find out," Alpha stated.

I nodded my head in agreement and replied, "Yeah, that was some freaky shit! We need to find out how he broke the protection ring around the perimeter. Also, call Pops and tell him to get everyone here. I know he is with Zontae and Mesa. I couldn't before because I heard you fighting in here and was worried about the babies. Syren and I had to make sure you all were okay."

"Some crazy ass shit happened in here, bruh, and I don't like it either. I don't play that shit about hurting babies and women," Alpha replied.

"Yeah, you damn right. Let's go check on Syren and the babies. At least I know they are safe in Nichelle's room," I responded.

Alpha nodded his head and said, "Let me call Pops, and I will meet you in there."

I left him in the room and went down the hallway to Nichelle's room. I said the words that would allow me in, and the door opened. I came across the girls in the bassinet first, and they were sleeping soundly. It made me wonder where baby Zaire was. I left the sitting area and saw Syren on the bed and baby Zaire playing with her hair.

When I got to her, she was ashen, and I could tell something was wrong. I moved baby Zaire into the bassinet with the girls and rushed back to Syren.

"Syren! Can you hear me? Syren!" I yelled, shaking her.

I looked all over her body and finally came across the deep gashes on her legs and noticed the bed at the bottom was full of blood. Why the hell wasn't she healing?

I didn't even think. I bit into my wrist and started pouring blood into her mouth. I had to massage her throat to get the first of it down. She still wasn't moving. I looked at her wound and saw that it was healing slowly. I kept giving her blood until I started getting woozy. I couldn't stop; I had to save Syren.

"Bruh, what the fuck are you doing?" Alpha yelled as he came into the room.

He tried to pull me off her, and I wouldn't budge.

"She needs blood; something is wrong, and she's not healing! I found her like this," I explained, trying to stay upright.

"Damn. Alright, lay down beside her man. I got it," Alpha stated.

He helped me lay down beside her. I blacked out for a moment, and when I came to, Alpha had his wrist to Syren's mouth, and her color was back to the milk chocolate brown that it normally was. I eased up and saw that her leg had completely healed, and her throat was moving on its own now.

"I think you can stop now; she looks a lot better. Plus, we don't have anyone here to feed on right now, so we need to conserve what reserves we have left. Did you call Pops?" I asked.

"Yeah. He is going to grab Zontae and the crew, and they are flashing here now. I wish I knew what happened to Syren. It's strange that she wasn't healing. Do you think it has anything to do with that strange shit that Luke had going on?" Alpha questioned as he sealed the wound on his wrist.

I looked down at Syren and moved the hair away from her face. She was so beautiful. I had wanted to talk to her before, but once my brother and her started speaking, I just figured he was more of her type than I was. He was the ladies' man, and I was the more reserved brother.

"It could be. Hell, I have no clue what happened. I just know that she was close to death when I came in here," I replied.

The door slammed open, and Zontae and the crew came flooding in.

"Where are my babies!" Mara yelled as she ran in.

"They are all in the bassinet. They are okay as far as we can tell, but I would have Nichelle scan them just to be sure," I replied.

Zontae grabbed Zaniyah while Mara grabbed Zaire. Mesa had Mena, and Lene was checking her out.

Nichelle walked in with another woman and said, "Put the babies back in the bassinet so that I can examine them. Alpha and Omega, tell us what happened. Your Pops, Slice, Zaidan, Draven, and Bayou are checking the breech to see what happened to the guards that were supposed to be patrolling that section. This is Dana."

I nodded at the lady. Since Alpha was there first, he caught everyone up on what went down in the nursery. I was rubbing Syren's hand, waiting on Nichelle to finish examining the babies so she could check her out as well.

"My mother wasn't with him?" Zontae asked.

I shook my head 'no' and replied, "Naw, it was another guy with dreads with him that I fought. He was either a shifter or a vampire. Jazz was with them too, but that was it."

"Oh no!" Nichelle said as she examined baby Zaire.

"Mama, what's wrong with my baby?" Mara asked.

Nichelle looked up with tears in her eyes.

"He put the Forbidden Book in their baby, didn't he?" Dana asked.

Nichelle nodded 'yes' and replied, "Yes, in my grandson. I smell the black magic around his mouth.

Dana ran over, and her eyes turned white. She placed her mouth over baby Zaire's.

"What the hell are you doing!" Zontae ran over before Nichelle stopped him.

"She isn't harming him. Watchers are balanced with black and white magic. She can sense things that I can't because my magic is white," Nichelle explained.

Dana's eyes mixed with black and white while she inhaled from baby Zaire, who stared at her with his hazel eyes. She finally stopped and shook her head.

"I have good and bad news. The good news is that most of the Forbidden Book is gone from his body. The bad news is that means Luke has one of the most powerful forms of magic in his body," Dana explained as she handed baby Zaire to Zontae.

"Wait a minute. You said most; does that mean that some of that evil shit is still in my baby?" Mara asked.

Dana hung her head and replied, "Believe me, you want that amount in there. If Luke had taken it all, then your baby would be dead. What's strange is he seems fine. Getting the book out would have meant sucking the life force out of him too. I smell white magic in him as well. Did a sorceress perform the breath of life spell on him?"

A light bulb went off in my head.

"That's what happened to Syren! I came in, and she had bled out, because her wound didn't heal. I didn't think it was anything else. Alpha and I gave her some blood, and her wound ended up healing, and her color came back," I explained.

Nichelle came over and scanned her niece.

"Um, you said that you and Alpha shared your blood with her? How much blood did you share?" Nichelle asked as she scanned Syren along with Dana.

Alpha replied, "Hell, a lot. She almost drained Omega, and I stepped in and gave her the rest, which was a lot, because she still didn't have her full color."

I nodded in agreement, and Nichelle came over and stared at both of us.

"She must have breathed her magic into baby Zaire, because it's gone from her body. She has something else in her body now. You might have saved her life, but you have also complicated it," Nichelle said.

"Why would we be complicating her life by saving her?" Alpha questioned.

My pops had just come in, and he replied, "Because, your dumb asses both gave her your blood and a lot of it. She will awaken a full-blooded succubus and very hungry. Unlike Samara, who's only part succubus because her Phoenix blood is her primary power, Syren will be all succubus, which is very dangerous if she isn't controlled. Not to mention, you both now share one mate. Syren belongs to both of you."

I stood there in shock. How did I fuck up this bad? I had completely forgot that sharing that amount of blood would cause the mating bond.

"Hold the fuck up! How the hell do you expect me to share a woman with my brother?" Alpha asked.

My Pops smiled and replied, "It's not like you and your brother haven't shared a woman before. I have heard the stories. The difference this time is she will be your mate. The good thing is, she will be a succubus, so she will definitely be able to keep up."

"That shit is not funny, Zeus! Your sons have basically turned my innocent niece into a polygamist and sex maniac! How the hell am I going to tell her this once she wakes up? Hell, what are you boys going to tell her brother Zoom when he finds out!" Nichelle ranted.

"Well, we have time. The conversion to a succubus takes three days. Once she wakes up, she will need to feed for the first twenty-four hours. So, boys, you need to get your rest. You have a wife to attend to, and I need to brush up on how to help my new daughter-in-law," Zeus replied.

Alpha and I both stared at each other. I didn't know how in the hell we would deal with having to share a mate together. Sure, we had shared hoes before, but never someone that we both were really interested in. I already knew that we were both feeling Syren. I didn't know how this triangle would end up. Would Syren just choose to be with one of us, leaving the other one heartbroken and bitter? Or would I end up battling my brother for Syren's heart or would sharing be a real option?

ZONTAE

This was some crazy shit about Syren, but I had my own problems to deal with, and the Syren issue couldn't be solved until she woke up in three days anyway.

"Omega and Alpha, you take Syren into the spare master bedroom down the hall. You both stay there and watch over her. That will give your pops time to look in the archives and figure some things out about your situation. Everyone else, let's head downstairs to come up with a plan to deal with Luke and Esha," I ordered.

Omega scooped up Syren, and Alpha held the door open for him.

"I am bringing the babies down with us in the bassinets. I don't trust leaving them alone right now," Mara stated.

I kissed her on the forehead, trying to ease some of the tension in her face.

"Alright, baby, we can do that," I replied.

Zeus grabbed the bassinet, and we all followed him downstairs into the family room where Santonio, Monroe, and the remaining members of the council were. A few were talking on their phones and pacing.

Santonio stood up and stared at Nichelle. He walked over to her and kissed her with so much passion that I was tempted to offer them a room. He finally came up for air.

"I had to do that because I missed you. But, I am pissed the fuck off that you would give me something to make me forget not only you, but my children. Do you know how many years I have missed out on from my daughters' lives? They are grown now with children of their own, Nichelle. I missed it all, and it was all because of you. I love you, but I don't know how to forgive you for that," Santonio stated.

Nichelle wiped tears from her eyes and replied, "I did it to protect you and our children. I never meant to hurt any of you. I know you need time; just make sure you take that into consideration. I love you, Santonio."

He nodded his head and walked over to Lene and Mara and gave them hugs.

"I'm sorry I wasn't there for you. Believe me, I wanted to be. I love you both so much. I want us to spend some time together so I can get to know the both of you and my grandchildren," Santonio said.

"It's okay, Dad. I felt the same way when I found out everything. Just take your time and keep an open mind. When you feel like you are ready, then listen to Mama's story," Mara stated.

Santonio nodded his head slowly and replied, "I will in my own time. I hate to cut this short, but I still am not 100 percent. Is there somewhere I can lay down at?"

Nichelle reached for Santonio, but he held his hand up, stopping her.

"Please, Santonio. Let me examine you and see if you are okay," she said.

Santonio shook his head 'no.' "Naw, Nichelle. I have had enough of you and your magic messing with me. I will be alright until I can get someone else to look at me. Selene, can you take me to a room where I can rest?"

"Yeah, Dad. I can do that. Babe, I will be right back," Lene said to Mesa and left with her father.

"Dana, I need to ask. What will happen to my son with him having some of the Forbidden Book in him?" I asked.

That was the main question that had been running through my mind since I heard it upstairs.

"I don't know. I wish I could tell you that it won't affect him, but that would be a lie. I can say that it's only a small amount. Syren put all her white magic into him, and that's very strong. Not to mention, the Phoenix blood and Incubus blood he has running through him. That should help counteract any effects it might have in him. I say watch him closely, and if you sense anything that's not normal, contact me or Nichelle," Dana explained.

Kaidan came over quickly to me and said, "I don't mean to interrupt, King Zontae, but we have a serious problem."

"Alright. Let's get settled down so that we can hit this shit head on," I stated.

We all sat down around the room and put the babies within reach. Selene had come back in, and she formed a soundproof bubble around them so that we could hear them but they couldn't hear us. They had been through enough today.

"Okay, Kaidan. What's going on besides finding Esha and Luke before they destroy the world?" I questioned.

Kaidan looked over at me with eyes that told me some shit had went all wrong.

"King Zontae, I hate to inform you, but the council has been breached. Angel and Dantez have sided with Queen Esha. I just learned that Angel and his spirits have invaded the Fae realm, and Dantez and his Seraphim have invaded the Rire realm and attacked Draven's people. That has declared all-out war against anyone that sides with you, especially since we announced that we voted to make you king instead of your mother," Kaidan explained.

This was news to me. I heard Kaidan call me King Zontae, but I didn't really pay it any mind.

"After the shooting, we noticed that Angel and Dantez had disappeared. We didn't know if they had been kidnapped or what. So, we did a majority vote, and you were voted in. Sorry. It looks like any type of coronation ceremony will have to wait," Kaidan answered.

I nodded my head in understanding. My celebration would be watching Luke's blood flow and Esha taking her last breath.

"No problem. We have bigger things to worry about. Look, I think you and Draven should go back to your realms and protect your people. We can convene when we get things under control. I appreciate your support, but your kingdoms need you more right now," I stated.

Slice had just gotten off his phone and walked over to us.

"I have some news. It looks like Esha and Luke have parted ways. One of the Dynasty Boyz is a Shadow and was able to follow them after they left. He tried to follow Esha after they broke off, but she used some kind of cloaking spell to hide her trail. That's not all either; the Waterlands and Shifter realm were just attacked as well. Monster, bruh, I hate to tell you this, but they have kidnapped your mate," Slice reported.

Monster jumped up and flashed away before anyone could say a word.

This was an all-out war on my supporters and the Underworld.

"Damn, that's fucked up. Slice, do you need to go with your brother and help him find his mate?" Mesa asked.

Slice shook his head 'no' and replied, "No. I am the king's bodyguard, and it is my job to be by his side to protect him. This could very well be a ploy to get me to separate from him so that they can make an attempt on his life. My brother is more than capable of finding his mate and restoring order to the shifter realm," Slice replied.

I nodded my head at Slice because I knew that he took his job very seriously. To be selected to guard the king was one of the highest honors in the Underworld. It made it all that more special with him being our cousin.

"Kings Draven, Kaidan, and Bayou, I appreciate your support, but you need to report to your kingdoms and protect your people. Please report to me soon about your situations while we find Luke and Esha and hopefully stop them for good," I stated.

Draven, Kaidan, and Bayou stood and bowed, flashing away. I felt bad that my mother had literally started a war in the Underworld and broke the council apart within the process. My uncle's phone buzzed, and he excused himself.

That left Nichelle, Mara, Lene, Mesa, Dana, and Monroe sitting in the family room. After hearing the shit that went down today at my house, I knew that Luke had to go before he could get to our children again. Plus, he had the Forbidden Book in him, and that was some shit that I couldn't let him use against the world.

"We are going after Luke first. Right now, he is the deadliest threat. My one problem is, how do we get the book out of him, or how do we kill him with the book inside of him?" I questioned.

Dana looked thoughtfully and replied, "I am thinking back on something that Alpha told us. He said that Luke was crying blue blood and had it coming from his nose. I think that the Forbidden Book is rejecting his body. My guess is, he will try and find a way to make his body accept the power. That also means that although he can tap into its power, he doesn't have full control of it, so we have to be very careful. The Forbidden Book's powers are nothing to laugh at. We need someone who has practiced black magic. Although I have both in my blood, I am no match for the book."

I thought for a minute, and I cursed under my breath, because I knew two people that dabbled in black magic, but I didn't know if I could fully trust them, especially not around my mate.

"Naw, bruh. I see that look on your face and don't even think about it. There is no way in hell we can trust them, especially not around our mates!" Mesa responded.

Selene looked between us both and said, "Wait... are you two talking about Dane and Devin? Those are the only two people that I know that practice black magic. If you are worried about Mara and me, we can take care of ourselves. The main thing is stopping Luke."

"Wait, my sons are dabbling in black magic! What the hell was Luke thinking!" Dana exclaimed.

We all stared at her, and she looked at us and shook her head in understanding.

"Right. It's Luke we are talking about. He already has my daughters worshipping Esha, so I shouldn't be surprised. Call them. We need them to trace Luke's magic; plus, I would like to speak with my sons," Dana replied.

"I got it, bruh. I need to set some things straight before they bring their asses over here," Mesa said and left the room.

Nichelle was staring at Monroe who had been unusually quiet.

"How did you survive? I thought you were dead along with Mason, your father?" Nichelle questioned.

He looked over at Dana, and she replied, "Esha sent me and Dantez to kill Mason and Monroe. When I saw that beautiful baby in the crib, I couldn't go through with it. I flashed over to the nearby farm and slaughtered a baby pig and spread the blood around the crib and the room. I hid Monroe with a friend of mine until about twenty years ago. Then I went to stay with them and told Monroe about his true heritage. I'm sorry, Nichelle, that I couldn't save Mason."

Nichelle stared at Dana and replied, "You were my closest friend, Dana, and it's hard for me to understand how you let Esha get away with so much without telling me."

Dana lowered her head and responded, "I messed up, Nichelle, but I was Esha's servant, and you know that I had to do whatever she said. I was in severe pain when I saved Monroe. I had to stay away for a few days, just so she wouldn't see. I finally found a way to break the bond when I saved the girls. But it meant me leaving my children behind with a monster. So believe me, I have suffered."

Nichelle stared at Dana and nodded her head.

"We have all suffered because of Esha and Luke. Hell, you don't think I want to spend some time with my mother and sisters? Fuck yeah, but we don't have time for that shit! We need to come together so that we can stop them for good. We can sort this other shit out later," Monroe stated.

We all nodded our heads in agreement. There were so many relationships that needed to be repaired. I wasn't sure how long it would take all of us, the Underworld, hell, the world to recover from the mess that Esha had started.

Mesa came back in and said that Dane and Devin were on their way.

"Dane and Devin had some info for us. It's not just the other realms that are being hit; all of them are being attacked. Even ours, bruh," Mesa stated.

"Fuck! They are trying to cause chaos so we get confused and don't go after them, or they want us to spread ourselves thin. We need to protect the clan but also take care of Luke. We need Zoom back here," I replied.

Mara walked over to me and sat in my lap.

"Zontae, Lene and I can take care of the problems here while you go after Luke. That way, we won't be anywhere near Dane and Devin, which will be one less thing you have to worry about," Mara stated.

I looked at her like she had lost her damn mind.

"The fuck I will leave you here by yourself! Who is going to protect our babies while you running around playing Miss Super Hero? I don't doubt you can protect yourselves, don't get me wrong, because I have seen you in action, but what happens if you use too much of your energy? Who will be there to protect you then?" I questioned.

Before she could answer, Monroe spoke up and replied, "I will. I will stay here and watch my sisters' backs while they protect your clan. I will make sure they don't overextend themselves. I would die before I let any harm come to them; you can believe that!"

"I don't trust anyone else with my grandbabies now. Plus, my husband is not well. I will stay here and protect the babies and Santonio. Not to mention Syren, who we have no clue what her condition is until she wakes up. I will also be here if the girls need any type of treatment or help. The girls are almost fully trained, and they are very powerful in their own right. They are the Queen and Princess of the Underworld; allow them to do their jobs, which is to help you and Mesa protect the kingdom. Don't underestimate them," Nichelle stated.

I looked at Mesa, and he reluctantly nodded in agreement. I grabbed my mate's face in my hands and pressed my lips to hers, savoring the taste of her that was unique to Mara. When I pulled back,

I had to discreetly adjust myself. Of course, that made Mara smile deviously.

"I swear, if you feel that you can't handle the situation, you call me right away. I'm not playing with you, Mara," I said.

Mara nodded her head and replied, "I will. I promise. Plus, Alpha and Omega will still be here at the house to help with protecting the babies."

"Okay. That means Dana, Devin, Dane, Slice, and Uncle Zeus will go with Mesa and me. We will hunt down Luke and take care of his ass. It's way past time for him to die," I replied.

The players were all set in their positions. Now it was time to end the game.

LUKE

$\mathcal{M}$y body felt like it was on fire! The moment Syren made me break contact with that baby, I had felt that something was wrong. That bitch had no right interfering in the exchange. I was going to suck that little bastard dry and smile when Zontae and Samara found his body.

I sat scratching my burning, itching skin, wondering when the side effects of the book would go away. My blood had turned bluish-black, and my skin kept changing from brown to black. My muscles kept expanding painfully and then would go away. I wiped more blue blood away from my nose.

"Dad, are you alright?" Jazz asked.

I smiled at Jazz who had always been a daddy's girl. I heard the talk about her spreading her legs for every man in the Underworld and the human world, but she was still my baby.

"I'm okay, baby. How are you feeling? I promise I am going to make her suffer for laying hands on my baby," I said.

Jazz smile and replied, "It's alright, Dad. I sliced up her leg pretty good. Plus, we need to figure out what's wrong with you. I thought that once you had the Forbidden Book, you would be invincible. This looks painful, Dad. I think you should call somebody and get some help. I don't think that you can handle the book being in your body."

Before I could stop myself, I back handed Jazz, and she went flying across the room and hit the wall.

I leapt over to her and reached down to help her up. When she flinched, I felt like shit.

"Jazz, baby, I am so sorry! I didn't mean to hit you; it just happened!" I tried to reason with her.

She had a frightened look on her face that I had never seen directed at me before. Then she replied in a shaky voice, "Daddy, I don't want you to keep the book in your body. You have never hit me before! It's making you sick and violent, Daddy! Please, get rid of it before it takes over completely, and there will be none of you left!"

I felt a sudden wave of anger and hostility toward Jazz. A voice in my head said, *how dare she ask you to get rid of the Forbidden Book! She is jealous of the power that you have now, and she needs to die! She is holding you back anyway with these punk ass feelings that you have for her. What the fuck do you need a daughter for? She is worthless as fuck unless she is opening her legs or her mouth! She is dead weight and holds no purpose for our mission to take over the world!*

I shook my head, trying to get rid of my dark thoughts. I loved Jazz, and I didn't know where those thoughts were coming from. I wish that she had left with Vice earlier, and she would be safe from me and the book.

"Jazz, you have to leave. Something is happening to me that I can't control. I don't want it to hurt you. I think you should call your sister and meet up with her and Esha; it might be safer until I get myself under control," I explained.

Jazz eased herself up and stared at me and responded, "Daddy, I don't want to leave you. Please, let me help you! You said that you didn't get all the book in you. Maybe once you have the whole book, you can control it. I know everybody thinks I'm dumb, but I can get the baby for you."

I shook my head 'no,' but the voice in my head was whispering, *yes, let her do it!* But, I knew it was a suicide mission. We might have gotten in once, but we wouldn't be able to get into Nichelle's house again.

"I can't let you do that, Jazz. You would die before you could even make it out of there. I am sure that those babies are guarded from all sides now. Please, do what I told you to do, and go and be with your sister," I demanded.

The burning intensified in my body. I could literally feel the blood burning in my veins. There was a pounding in my head, and the voice was getting stronger. My muscles were stretching to the point where they felt like they were about to snap. There was a roaring in my ear, and all the sensations toned down.

I didn't know how much more I or my body could take of the pain without literally dying or going crazy. A thought popped in my head, and I remembered that there was an old witch that lived in Pegram. She had been around even before I was born. She also was rumored to have dabbled in the dark arts, more specifically Forbidden Magic, which was where the book originated.

"Look, Jazz. I love you, and I will send for you as soon as I get this under control. I just need you to stay safe, baby. Daddy loves you so much. Now leave and call Jade and tell her that you are meeting up with them. Make sure she knows that I love her and Esha. I will be coming to claim my family as soon as I have all of the powers of the book," I stated.

Jazz looked at me sadly with tears in her eyes and replied, "Okay, Daddy. I hate to leave you alone and in pain, but if you want me to, I will go. Just please promise me that you won't die on me; you are all that I have."

I hugged Jazz tightly and kissed her on the head. I would miss her, but it was for her own good. The Forbidden Book was unpredictable, which made me unpredictable.

Jazz dropped her arms and stepped away from me while wiping her eyes. She turned away and left out of the room. As soon as I heard the front door close, I snapped my fingers and pulled up the tome with the list of witches in the area. I had to flip back to the very first sections placed in the book. Mary Turner was her name, and she was rumored to have a cabin deep in the woods of Pegram. I needed to go now and find out what she knew.

I no longer flashed since I was the book. I appeared in the woods in Pegram and followed the trail of dark magic. She would cooperate, or she would suffer until she did.

I was almost to the end of the trail of darkness, and the voices in my head were telling me that we were close. The book was sensing the dark magic, and I could feel my body pulsing with excitement. I looked up as I rounded the corner, and there was a two-story log cabin in front of me with a wraparound porch.

An older light-skinned black lady with long gray hair was sitting on the porch in a rocking chair. I could sense her powerful magic from here. I started toward her and hit a force field that knocked me back into a tree.

"Hello, Luke. I have been expecting you. My name is Mary. Go ahead and state your business. I grow tired and wish to sleep soon," Mary stated.

I didn't like this old bitch. All I wanted from her wrinkled up old ass was her magic and for her to tell me how to control the Forbidden Book in my body. I had to get her to let her guard down so that I could accomplish my goals.

I put on my best smile and replied, "Wouldn't it be better if I sat with you and stated my business? You just have to take the shield down."

Mary laughed and replied, "Why would I do that? So that you could kill me by sucking me dry of my power? I don't think so, young man. Now, you are messing with my patience, and believe me, you don't want to do that."

She stared at me with cold black eyes, and I knew that she meant every word she said. Not to mention, I felt the power surge in the air around me, letting me know that she was preparing to retaliate if I tried anything.

"Fine. I am here to speak with you about the Forbidden Book. The legend says that you once possessed the Forbidden Book in your body for years and that you have lived where others have died. How did you survive?" I asked.

Mary stared at me as if she was examining me, with a smile that sent chills down my spine. The voices of the book hissed in my head and were whispering to kill her because she was an enemy. It was almost as if the book feared the witch.

"I will not tell you how to control the book, Luke, because you possess the Forbidden Book in your body. You are not worthy of that type of magic, but you took it anyways. There are very few that can control the book, and you are not one of them. Your soul is black with hatred and greed. The book will devour your soul and existence," Mary stated.

I sneered at her and responded, "What the fuck are you talking about? It's black magic! Black magic is evil and meant to be used for evil! It should love me because I am dedicated to destroying the Underworld and taking over the planet. The Forbidden Book will help me rule!"

Mary laughed so hard she almost fell out of the rocker she was seated in.

"That is a common misconception. Black magic is not meant for evil. Its use depends on the person wielding it. It is beyond powerful and can be used to destroy the world. That is why only a few people are meant to wield it. You are not one of those people. You have made a grave mistake by taking it into your body. Even now, it is eating away at your very being like a parasite. You are doomed, and you deserve everything that you are about to get. Your fate was sealed as soon as you welcomed it into your soul. I hope you die a slow and painful death. Now leave so I may sleep. You make my ass hurt just feeling the book eating you alive and laughing at your dumb ass," Mary stated as she got up from the chair to go into the cabin.

This was not the way I pictured this shit going. Why wasn't she listening to me and helping? She was supposed to understand my plight and give me the information that I needed and shut the hell up and let me drain her old ass dry.

I gathered all the power within me to strike at the shield and get to this old bitch! My skin turned black and my muscles bulged, and the veins were popping up in my forearms. I felt the dark blue blood running from my nose and my eyes. I lifted my arms and the power from the book, as well as my own magic, came to me. I poured all that magic into a huge power ball that was black with streaks of lightning through it. I drew my arms back like I was about to pitch a baseball, concentrating on the weakest part of the shield. I threw it and hit the blue force field, burning a hole straight through it.

"You not saying shit now, are you, you old bitch!" I yelled as I floated through the opening toward Mary.

Surprisingly, she just stood there and waited for me to float to her with a smile on her face. I smiled because her smart ass was about to die, and I was going to suck her powers out of her for my own use and pleasure. It made my dick hard thinking about it.

I went for her throat with my hands, and they went right through her body as if she were a ghost or spirit.

"What the fuck!" I yelled in confusion.

Mary cackled as she stared at me and responded, "You are one dumb ass motherfucker to think that I would make it easy for you to kill me and take my powers! Now get your degenerating ass out of here before I melt the skin from your bones! I have more important guests to attend to tonight, and you have a date with death!"

She wavered away into nothing along with the cabin. The old bitch had tricked me! She was never here, and according to her, there was no way to stop the book from taking over my body. Fuck her. I could control the book! Bitch was probably jealous that I had all the power and she didn't. I would take the Duvalls down with my newly acquired powers, then there would be no one to stop me!

JAZZ

J closed the door to my father's safe house, after I waited for him to leave, and cried. There was no way that I was letting him suffer. If he needed that ugly ass baby, then I would snatch his ass up and bring him to die. Hell, Mesa should have chosen me, and Zontae should have chosen my sister. Those babies should have been our babies!

Well, now I had to come up with a plan to kidnap Zontae's son and bring him to my daddy. Maybe a little accident could happen to Mesa's little bundle of joy too.

I smiled as I walked away from the house.

MESA

*W*e were all gathered out front, waiting on dumb and dumber to get here. I wasn't happy that we had to depend on them to do shit because their asses were still sniffing after our mates. I didn't trust them, that was why I told Lene to keep her ass in the house. I didn't want him to be staring at her and end up with his eyeballs shoved up his ass on accident or something.

"Why they taking so fucking long? You would think they would be running here wanting to meet their mama. Not to mention, their psycho daddy is running around here with Pandora's Box in his fucking guts. I just want to get this shit over with and kill his ass so I can get back here to my wife and daughter. I don't trust our no-good backstabbing mama not to attack while we are gone," I stated.

Zontae and Uncle Zeus both nodded their heads in agreement.

Before Zontae could answer, Devin and Dane appeared in front of us.

I was feeling some type of way instantly because Devin's ass was looking all around like he was expecting Lene to be there.

"Yo, what the fuck are you looking all around for, or should I say who! My mate isn't here, so you wasted that Crisco in your hair, motherfucker! The only woman you should be looking for is your mama that you haven't even met! Get your mind right before I get that shit right for you," I stated, getting in Devin's face.

He stepped to me like he wanted to try me, but Zeus stepped in between us.

"Look, we don't have time for this shit. Luke has a head start, and we need to find him and stop him before it's too late. Y'all can measure dicks later. Now suck that shit up and let's find this motherfucker," Zeus said.

I bunched my face up at Uncle Zeus and replied, "Man, Unc, don't ever mention dicks and sucking shit up when it's a whole bunch of motherfuckers with dicks swinging in attendance. That shit don't sound right."

We all burst out laughing until Dana walked over, and Dane and Devin met their mother for the first time. I stepped to the side and let them have their moment. It was bittersweet because it reminded me that my own mama wasn't shit but a power-hungry bitch.

I felt a touch on my arm and looked up to find Nichelle standing beside me with a small smile on her face.

"Your mate sensed your mood and wanted me to check on you. She knew that with Devin and Dane here, you wouldn't want her to come out, so I volunteered to come out and check on you. What's wrong, son?" Nichelle asked.

Just hearing her say that one word made me feel like I at least had a mother-in-law and a mate that cared about my wellbeing.

I smiled and placed my hand on hers and replied, "I'm cool, Mama Nichelle. I just have my moments sometimes. Tell Lene I am alright and to kiss my baby girl for me. Hopefully, we will be leaving soon so I can get this stalking ass roach away from my mate. No matter how many times we get rid of these motherfuckers, they just keep coming back!"

Nichelle laughed and responded, "Don't worry, Mesa. They won't ever get near my girls again. You just worry about finding Luke. Now, before I leave, let me just say that it's okay to think about your mother and wish she was different. You love her, Mesa, and she will always be your mother. Just know that if you ever feel lacking in that department, you always have me."

Nichelle smiled and flashed away. I smiled and looked up and saw my brother smile and give me a head nod. I guess I wasn't the only one feeling some type of way about our mama. I guess it was because we knew her days were numbered because of her actions.

Zontae, Zeus, and I walked over and listened to Dana catch her sons up on why she had left. From what I was seeing, Devin was understanding, but Dane, not so much.

"Did you ever think about your children that you left behind? I mean, we just found out that we had sisters! You knew what kind of monster that Luke was, and you just left us with his crazy ass! Maybe your daughters wouldn't have turned out to be such conniving whores if you had stuck your ass here instead of worrying about somebody else's children!" Dane yelled.

Smack!

Dana smacked the shit out of Dane and replied, "Don't ever talk about your sisters like that! I don't give a damn what they have done! From what I hear, your hands aren't so clean either, son. Now you have every right to be mad at me for the choices that I have made. We each have our own destinies that we must follow. Unfortunately, mine meant leaving my children behind, whom I loved with all my heart. Believe me, I thought your father wouldn't include his own children in his dark plans."

Dane scoffed and replied, "You can save that destiny shit for someone who believes in that shit! My destiny was to be with Samara, and you see how that fucking worked out! She is mated to Zontae and has his babies! I was supposed to grow up with a mother and father who loved me and taught me the ways to rule as the King of the Magic Realm, but that's all gone to hell now that my father has merged with the Forbidden Book! My life is ruined because of the choices that you and my father have made. So forgive me if I am not running into your opened arms, Mother!"

Zontae moved toward Dane with a deadly look in his eyes and

said, "Keep my mate's name out your mouth. She wasn't before and never will be yours. Your ass was delusional!"

Zontae and Dane stood there in a stare-off while Dana stood there with tears in her eyes. My uncle Zeus walked over to her and placed his arm around her. It dawned on me by the way he was looking at her, that she must be the woman he was talking about that he was in love with and Esha made her marry someone else.

"Dane, man, you can't talk to her like that. That's still our mama regardless of the situation. You don't have to like her, but you at least need to respect her. Now, tell them what we learned about Luke. Finding him is what we can all agree on right now," Devin stated, drawing Dane's attention away from Zontae.

Dane huffed and turned away from everyone, reaching in his pocket, pulling out a red crystal, and faced Zontae.

"Look, we have been hitting the tomes to find out ways that we could track Luke with the Forbidden Book in his body. There wasn't anything of use in them. However, there was a reference deep in the older tomes of a witch that used to possess the Forbidden Book in her body and survived. We need to find her and see if she can give us any information on how we can find Luke and destroy the Forbidden Book," Dane explained.

Dana screamed out in pain, grabbing her chest. "Ahhhhh!"

Zeus gathered her in his arms and asked, "Dana, what's wrong?"

We all waited for the answer as she stood up.

"I haven't had visions for a decade, but I have an overwhelming feeling of doom and death if we follow this path to the old witch. I feel it settling in my chest. It's a hot burning sensation that feels like it's ripping my heart in two. We must find another way to stop Luke. The witch means death!" Dana yelled.

"Man, fuck naw! Did her ass just say death? Now, I ain't no punk, but if she is supposed to be a watcher and she sees death, don't you think we should listen to her? I got a mate and a daughter I need to come home to. If you think you are taking me to some old ass witch so she can kill me and you come back for Lene, you got another thing coming! My dead dick ass will be right back here from the grave to kill your ass and lay dead dick down to Lene. Fuck with it if you want to!" I screamed, getting in Devin's face.

I didn't trust neither one of these motherfuckers, and this plan sounded shady as hell. They really might be setting us up to die. If we were out of the way, they could have Lene and Mara all to themselves.

Devin turned back around and responded, "I am not going to lie and say that I don't love Lene, but I hate my father more. He knew that messing with the Forbidden Book would doom our family, and he didn't give a fuck about us. I swear on my life that the information that Dane just shared is the truth. It was the only thing that we could find that had any truth to it. Now either you can trust us or go at this shit alone! Bottom line, point blank period! My brother and I will handle my father while you all go off chasing your tails, letting him get away; or you end up dying, trying to go up against a magical force that you have no clue on how to stop—your choice!"

I stared at him for a moment and then punched his ass dead in the throat. He immediately grabbed his neck, trying to catch his breath. His mama ran over to him, trying to help him. His brother tried to walk up on me, but Zeus put a stop to that and pulled him back. He mean-mugged me with his blue eyes glowing and turned to see about his brother.

"Damn, Mesa, he was making sense. You didn't need to hit his ass," Zontae said, walking over to me.

I laughed and replied, "Hell, I know that. That's not why I hit his stupid ass. It was his delivery that got his ass hit in the throat! Raising his voice and shit like he was going to do something."

After Devin got up and was halfway breathing, we decided the brothers' plan was the best one we had right now.

"Now, we will cast the spell to locate the old witch. Unfortunately, we have to use our black magic to do so. We know that it's forbidden on your grounds, so I need your permission to use it, King Zontae, especially since we are already on thin ice for using it," Dane stated, looking at Zontae for confirmation.

Zontae nodded, and Dane put the red crystal on the ground. Devin joined his brother, and their eyes turned sapphire blue. Devin pulled out a dagger and sliced the palm of his hand and squeezed the blood onto the red crystal on the ground, where the drops of blood sizzled like frying bacon in a skillet. He passed the dagger to Dane, and he repeated the process. They both lifted their hands in the air, and Dane started chanting.

"Tenebris spirituum exaudi me! Hoc sacrificium nostrum!" Dane chanted in Latin.

The sounds of nature around us quieted, and black clouds started rolling in over our heads. A swirling circle formed over our heads in the center of the clouds with red in the middle and lightning. It crackled with each strike.

"I call upon the dark forces and my ancestors to aid me in our quest. Your servants need your guidance to send us on the path of the one who served you well in the past, the Black Witch!" Dane yelled at the center.

Lightning shot from the clouds into the crystal on the ground, turning the dull red to a glowing red beacon. The clouds abated, and everything around us returned to normal. Dane and Devin's eyes changed back to brown, and Devin picked up the glowing red crystal and placed it around his neck. As soon as it touched his skin, it glowed brighter and lifted, turning toward the right, painting a path of red into the distance.

"The path has been revealed. Time to go and see the one they call the Black Witch," Dane stated.

Dane and Devin flashed down the red lighted path followed by Dana. Zeus, Zontae, and I looked at each other and flashed behind them, down the path that mirrored the color of blood. I just prayed that our blood wouldn't be mingled with it by the time this was all over.

MARY (THE BLACK WITCH)

$\mathcal{I}$ walked around my cabin getting everything prepared for the arrival of my next guests. This day was a long time coming and had been in the making for a decade now.

"Mama Mary, I made sure to get everything ready in the kitchen just like you asked me to. Do you need anything else before I go for my run?" Lawrynn asked.

I smiled at her, hating that I would soon lose her companionship. I loved her like a daughter and wanted nothing but the best for her. What started out as a way to atone for my sins, ended up being the best thing that ever came into my life. Lawrynn was my second chance at being a better mother than I had been to my own biological daughter.

"No, baby. You go ahead and get your exercise in before our guests arrive. Please make sure that you watch out for the hunters that are in the area. It's deer season and they have itchy trigger fingers," Mary stated.

Lawrynn laced up her tennis shoes and replied, "I will; don't worry. I am going to grab some of those mint leaves and sage that you love too, Mama Mary, while I am out. Love you!"

"Love you too, baby," I responded as she went out of the door.

Pulling the curtains back, I watched as Lawrynn stretched and prepared for her run. She had really grown into a beauty with her Hershey skin, beautiful oval, chocolate color eyes, and pouty lips. Her naturally thick and long hair was pulled into a ponytail. She was such a strong, loyal, and intelligent young woman, and I was so proud of what she had become despite her past. Her eyes changed to a greenish-yellow color, and she took off into the woods using her preternatural speed.

I said a protection spell over her, even though she was more than capable of taking care of herself. Lawrynn was a fully developed Kanima, a shifter that resembled a snake with legs and had venomous claws, tail, and bite. She has wings and was very powerful because she had the royal bloodline of her people running through her veins. She was one of a kind now, because her family had been wiped off the face of the planet by a cold-blooded killer who held no regard for life. I knew because I was that killer that killed her family and clan. The only reason she was alive was because her mother hid her beneath the porch with a servant that was protected by a cloaking spell. Trying to save the princess of their clan had cost her parents—the king and queen—their lives. The Most High brought her to me years later when I asked to be forgiven for my crimes. He also told me a secret about her that had me gasping. I would let her know when the time was right; not now. It wasn't time.

The Most High said I was to be her master and teach her the ways of the Underworld. But she ended up teaching me about forgiveness and being a better person. No longer my servant, she became my daughter instead, forgiving me for killing her people and accepting me as her mother. Our bond was strong, and I loved our relationship. I just hated that my hate and need for revenge caused her so much pain.

I shook my head in disgust, remembering how much devastation I had caused in the world with my greed, hatred, and jealousy. I allowed a man to dominate my thoughts and turn me into a monster. Allowing the Forbidden Book into my body while I was pregnant, only enhanced the pure evil that was in my heart. I never once thought about the effect that it would have on my soul, let alone my innocent child that I was carrying. I had not only sold my soul to the dark one; I had turned my child's pure heart black.

I closed my eyes and remembered Mathias, the man who started it all. He was the most handsome warrior that I had laid eyes on, until I saw his best friend, Elijah. I was by the river weaving baskets with my best friend, Nahla. Nahla and I were only born a day apart from each other and shared the gift of magic. Our mothers were best friends and were the first women that the Most High blessed with the gift of magic. They were both High Priestess, and we were training to become just like them and take our place in the dynasty. There were other clans among us—vampires, shifters, Fae, and many more. We all lived in Egypt amongst the humans in secret. The Most High said that they were not ready to know of our existence yet because they would not understand our gifts or be jealous or frightened by them. We all soon found out that he was right.

I was brought out of my reverie by the strong pull of black magic in the area. I looked at the clock, and I had been deep in my thoughts for about an hour. Lawrynn would be here soon along with my guests. Truths would be told today that would shed light on the darkness that was taking over and choking out the light in their lives. This was part of my atonement for my many sins that I had committed. This was my judgement day.

ZONTAE

We had followed the red path deep into the woods. The more we traveled, the brighter the red became. It was weird because it looked almost like blood flowing through veins. I was tempted to touch it because it was calling to the vampire side of me, but fuck that! It was no telling what it would do to me because it was created from dark magic.

"Man, do you two really know if this red shit knows the way to go? We have been following it for a while now. We need to find this bitch soon and kill Luke before he comes back for my nephew!" Mesa shouted at Devin.

That shit had my blood boiling and eyes turning red thinking about how Luke put that evil shit into my son. If Syren hadn't been there to stop him, he would have killed him by draining him dry. The bad part was, there was still some of it inside of my son. Did that mean that my son was part evil now? Would it harm him? I needed to find out the answers because I could sense Mara's fears along with my own. It was my job to protect and care for my family, and I was tired of slipping and failing them.

"Look, I want to get there as much as you do. You act like I know exactly where we are going. I am following this shit just like you.

What you need to do is stop bitching, because I am really getting tired of your shit!" Devin yelled, stepping into Mesa's face.

Dane grabbed his brother and pushed him back down the path and said, "Cut that shit out, Devin! We don't have time for that right now. Our dad is somewhere doing who knows what, and you trying to start a fight. Cut that shit!"

"Yeah, you better listen to your brother before I knock your hairline back in place! Your shit looks lopsided like a motherfucker! Like someone crayoned that motherfucker on!" Mesa yelled.

I shook my head and laughed because these two were going to kill each other before we found this witch. Hell, Dane wasn't my favorite person either, but I needed his ass so we could find Luke. My kingdom was in shambles right now, and there was no telling what Esha was up to while we were out here searching for Luke.

"All of you shut the hell up! We are hunting the most dangerous witch ever known, and she could have traps all throughout this forest to kill us. Now I don't know about you, but I don't want to die out here in bum fuck woods!" Dana yelled and headed down the path.

Uncle Zeus smiled and watched her ass switch from side to side as she stomped angrily down the path and stated, "You know that she is going to be my mate. I was cheated out of my chance with her before, but this time, I am not letting her get away. Instant divorce once I kill her fuck boy ass husband."

I laughed and replied, "You got that, Unc. Do what you have to do."

We laughed and followed everyone down the path. We had traveled another twenty minutes when something dropped from the trees and jumped on Dane's back.

"Ahhh! What the fuck!" Dane yelled, trying to throw it off his back.

The creature flew up into the sky after slashing its long glowing-green claws across Dane's face. Dane fell to the ground, paralyzed with a pained look frozen on his face. Devin rushed over to his brother along with Dana. They started checking out the deep red slashes on his check that were oozing blood and some type of glowing green liquid.

My eyes turned red and my fangs dropped, as I growled toward the figure in the sky. Mesa's and Zeus's claws and fangs extended as they circled the creature. It had yellow eyes with black slits like a snake. It was green with iridescent scales that shimmered as they ran down the very curvy body, so I could tell it was female; I just wasn't sure what it was. There was a long-pointed tail that glowed green also.

"You are trespassing! This is the territory of the Black Witch, and sorcerers are not allowed here, especially Harpers! Leave or die!" she hissed.

Devin's eyes turned dark blue as he looked up from his brother who was still frozen on the ground, and replied, "Bitch, I'm about to fuck you up! What the hell did you do to my brother?"

The thing in the sky replied, "You can try your luck if you want to, but I guarantee you that you won't make it out of here! Your mama will be burying two sons today!"

"Lawrynn, stop! These are the guests that I was preparing for. Now come down and prepare to meet them," said an old lady who appeared out of nowhere.

She had long white flowing hair with butter toffee skin. She was beautiful and somewhat familiar to me, which was strange because I had never seen her before. She smiled at me and then turned her attention to Lawrynn.

"But, you said the Harpers were enemies. Why are you welcoming them into your home, Mama Mary?" Lawrynn asked as she floated down to the ground.

Mary placed her hand on Lawrynn's scaly face and she instantly turned back into her naked human form. I had to turn my head to block out the sight.

"Damn!" Mesa mumbled walking backward toward me.

Little mama was beautiful, but I wasn't saying shit. Samara's crazy ass might pick up on that shit and set my dick on fire. Mary waved her hand, and Lawrynn now had clothes on; a pair of jeans and a white t-shirt.

"Lawrynn, go in the house and take my wards down. Our guests will be joining us for a discussion," Mary instructed.

Lawrynn looked unsure at Mary and turned to look at all of us with a silent threat in her eyes and finally flashed away.

"Yo, what the hell is she, and what the hell did she do to his corpse looking ass?" Mesa questioned while pointing down at Dane.

Mary walked over to Dane and replied, "Lawrynn is a Kanima, the one of the last of her kind. She is a warrior queen, so make sure that you respect her, or she will kill you. Her bite and scratches are poison to most kind. The only ones here that could be immune are yourself and your brother because of the Phoenix blood running through your veins from your mates. Dana and Devin, if you will allow me to give Dane the antidote, he should be fine in the next few minutes."

Dana looked strangely at Mary and finally nodded her head in agreement. Devin was about to argue, but Dana placed her hand on his shoulder to stop him.

Mary kneeled with a vial in her hand and tilted the contents into Dane's mouth. His body started twitching and then it stopped as his face healed, and he opened his eyes.

"What happened? Who are you?" Dane asked, slurring his words.

Mary smiled and looked over at Devin and stated, "Bring your brother into my cabin so we can all chat. We have a lot to cover before the battle begins."

Mary started walking toward a clearing, and suddenly, a cabin shimmered to life in front of us. We all walked behind her but were looking around on high alert. Hell, we were out here in the middle of no fucking where with a damn Kanima and the Black Witch who the damn devil was afraid of. I didn't know what this lady had up here sleeve or if she was an enemy or an ally.

We entered the cabin, and it was larger than it looked from the outside but was also more modern than I expected. She told us to have a seat in the living room, and we all found seats on the three large brown sofas she had in the room.

Lawrynn came into the room with an attitude and plopped down on the cushion that was in front of the fireplace and directly beside Mary. I just wanted to know how to kill Luke now that he had the Forbidden Book in his body. It was as if she knew what I was thinking. She stared at me and said, "I know why you are here. You want to know about the Forbidden Book and how to stop it, which will stop Luke also, correct?"

We all looked around at each other a little spooked because this lady had an eerie calm about her that had me a little shook. I could sense the power in her, and it made my demon uncomfortable. It was like she had a sweet façade on the outside and something deadly hiding on the inside. She was someone that I knew I had to watch carefully.

"You seem to know a lot about us, but all we know about you is that you are the Black Witch who once held the Forbidden Book in your body. Now, the question is, what do you want from us in order to get the information that we need?" I questioned because we didn't have time for the bullshit.

Mary gave a brief smile and replied, "I will give you the information. All I ask is that you hear me out and keep an open mind about what I have to tell all of you."

I frowned up and responded, "What would you need to speak with us about?"

"You need to know the history of the Forbidden Book and the effects that it has had and will have on your lives. If you don't know everything about your enemy, how can you defeat them?" Mary questioned.

I looked around at everyone and asked, "Is this cool with everyone?"

Mesa sighed and responded, "We came here for answers, so let's get this shit over with. No offense, but we got enemies to kill."

Everyone nodded in agreement, and I replied, "Ms. Mary, the floor is yours."

She nodded and replied, "My mother and her best friend were one of the original witches granted power by the Most High in Egypt. They trained my best friend Nahla and I in the ways of the white magic so that we could help mankind one day with our powers. We lived amongst the humans along with other kinds of Underworlders, but we all lived together in one big clan; not separated into different realms like it is now. Our mothers worked for the Pharaoh as healers, the shifters as guards, and the vampires as workers or advisors. We were in plain sight but tried to blend in with the humans as much as possible. The Most High felt that humans were not ready to be told of our existence."

"What does your history lesson have to do with the Forbidden Book? I mean, I agreed to listen, but so far I ain't heard nothing that tells me how to kill this asshole and burn that damn creepy ass book," Mesa stated.

I thought that Mary would be upset, but she just replied, "Patience, Mesa. Believe me, my story is the exact thing that you need to hear in order to defeat the enemy and head home to your daughter and son."

Mesa frowned up and responded, "I don't have a son. I have a daughter. Your visions must be off, because you got that one wrong."

Mary smiled and replied, "Did I? Are you sure? Hmm, very interesting. You might want to check on that one. Well, as I was saying, we lived peacefully together as one clan. That all changed the day that Nahla and I were at the river, and two new Underworlders arrived. They were best friends, Mathias who was a vampire, and his friend Elijah who was a sorcerer. I met Mathias first but fell in love Elijah. Elijah was sweet and loving, whereas Mathias was devious and deceptive. I tried to warn Nahla about the feelings that I sensed in him, but she was so in love with him that she wouldn't listen. One day, a temple worker went to get water from the river and found the Pharaoh's beloved daughter bloody and naked on the bank. Her throat had been ripped out and she was raped. It was gruesome and left the humans out for blood for the killer."

Tears dropped from her eyes as she told that part of the story. Lawrynn grabbed Mary's hand and squeezed it.

"Maybe you should get some rest, Madam Mary. You haven't been feeling well the past few days," Lawrynn stated.

Mary patted her cheek and replied, "No, child. I need to finish this story; lives depend on it."

"Okay, but if you feel like you need to rest, let me know, and I can uninvite your guests," Lawrynn said while giving Devin and Dane an evil look.

Mary nodded her head 'yes' and took a sip of bottled water that Lawrynn handed her.

"Thank you, child. As I was saying, the Pharaoh's daughter was found murdered, and that's when the chaos really began. The guards started searching high and low for her killer or killers. But a week went by and more human women were raped and murdered. In our clan, our mothers tried to find out which vampire was killing the women, but they were soon found murdered and raped just like the human women. Nahla and I were devastated. Elijah was there for me and promised that he would find her killer. The Most High came and told all the Underworlders that we needed to separate into different clans and spread out because we were a danger to the humans and each other. That meant that we couldn't mingle with anyone other than our own kind. He had created realms for each species. Nahla begged The Most High to not separate the Underworlders because that meant she couldn't be with Mathias because he was a vampire. Elijah was a witch, so he could stay. Many families were separated that day."

"My father told me about the Day of Separation. He lost his mother and a sister who were witches," Dana stated.

Mary nodded sadly and replied, "Yes, many were mad at the Most High because of his decision. I was one of them. We felt that he was being unfair in his judgement. But we did what we were told and planned for the separation. The night before the Day of Separation, Elijah came to me so that we could mate and be together. In the middle of the mating, I noticed something wrong because it became rough and forceful. The next thing I knew, Elijah's eyes turned green, and he changed into Mathias, and he bit me. It was Mathias raping me. He had taking a potion to temporarily look just like Elijah. I screamed, and Nahla and Elijah came running into the tent. Mathias said that I had seduced him into sleeping with me. Nahla and Elijah believed him and turned their backs on me. I ran from the clan that night and vowed vengeance on all of them. I turned to the dark arts and started studying them. I found out that Mathias had been beheaded a month later for the murders and rapes. But the news that devastated me the most was that I was pregnant by Mathias, and Elijah and Nahla were mated and expecting a child together as well. They had mated the day after I ran from the clan. To make matters worse, their bloodline was chosen to receive special gifts from the Most High. My heart turned black, and I created the Forbidden Book."

I just stared at her. Did she just say that she created the fucking Forbidden Book? The most evil thing ever created.

"Hold up, you created it!" Dane yelled.

Mary grimly nodded her head and replied, "Yes, I made a deal with the Dark One and traded my child's soul so that I could be powerful enough to make everyone that turned their backs on me pay. All I had was hate! Hate for my best friend and the love of my life, the humans, and most of all, hate for the thing that Mathias placed inside of me. I was the Dark One's warrior, and he used me to corrupt and destroy lives all for his pleasure. I killed Nahla and Elijah, leaving their newborn daughter to be raised as an orphan by her clan. Lawrynn and her people were part of that destruction. I killed the whole Kanima clan because of hate and the quest for more power. That's what he does. He makes you crave more power until you are sick and overrunning with darkness."

"How could you sell your daughter's soul? I get it, you were raped and wanted nothing to do with the child. Why not give her to someone who wanted her? I mean, this is crazy!" Dana yelled.

"Dana, you can't talk! You left us with the damn devil and didn't even look back!" Dane yelled.

"No, she's right, Dane. I did the most terrible thing a mother could do. I raised her to hate and destroy everything that Nahla's daughter loved. What I didn't know was that I was the one that was tricked by the Dark One. When I realized it, I went to the Most High and begged for forgiveness. Lawrynn was put into my care as part of my atonement. I didn't want my daughter to put that curse in her children, so I used a spell to protect my grandchildren by sacrificing my immortality. That's why I am aging," Mary stated.

"Enough! Your life was fucked up, and in turn, you fucked your child up! How is all of this going to help stop the Forbidden Book that Luke has inside of him?" I demanded.

"That's the thing, son. Luke only has a small portion of the Forbidden Book inside of him, just like your son and I do. The Dark One loves to trick people with promises of power just to pour his hate into your soul so he can devour it. He uses people to do his bidding, and you have no clue that you were tricked until it's too late. Luke fell for it just like I did. He was here earlier, and the book is already making him crazy. He wasn't meant to have it, so his body is starting to reject it. It will take over his mind and use the body until his body temp burns too high to take it, and he will die. Problem is, the Forbidden Book will go back into its last host, which is your son. That means he will start the same cycle of evil that my daughter is causing now," Mary explained.

My heart skipped a beat when she said that shit would go back into my son. This was my worst nightmare come true. My son was innocent and had only been alive a short time. If I had to sacrifice my life for his, I would.

"So how do we stop that from happening?" I asked.

"We have to kill my daughter and get the Forbidden Book to enter back into my body. The Most High did a blessing over my body that will trap it inside of me. Once it is inside of me, you must get Samara, Selene, and Mason to burn me alive to kill myself and the book. They are the ones combined that can destroy the book. It is their destiny, because Nichelle is Nahla and Elijah's daughter, and her children have been gifted by the Most High. Just like my daughter is the vessel that the Dark One used to pour all his evilness into. Your mother, Esha, is my daughter, and you and Mesa are my grandsons. Zontae and Mesa, Esha is the Forbidden Book.

"Fuck!" Mesa and I said at the same time.

PART II
"CHAOS"

"I'm not afraid to die if it means that my family will be safe. I will go down to hell and air that bitch out if I have to!"

— ZONTAE'

KING ZAIRE

*W*e were on our way to meet up with my sons at the Dynasty Boyz clubhouse. I was excited and nervous at the same time because I had no clue on how they would react to me. Zoom told me that Esha had killed Stone who was pretending to be me all these years. I mourned my friend and protector for giving his life for mine.

Dr. Phillips, or Lamont as he liked to be called by us now, was talking to Ever and Zoom about the tainted B-packs and the Underworlders that were being infected. We had decided to drive since Christy was with us, and she was having a hard time with finding out about the supernatural world and her mother. She was currently sitting in the back seat with them, pouting and typing furiously on her phone. Both girls were beautiful just like their mother, Ever, with her blonde hair and brown eyes, and Christy with her hazel eyes and blonde mixed with red hair. I could see Esha in their features. I just had no clue how my sons would react to their new sisters either. They had been through hell the past couple of weeks with all the secrets and betrayals being revealed, and here I came with more of the same.

"King Zaire, are you alright? I know that it can't be easy hearing everything that Esha has done to your sons and the Underworld. Not to mention, the human world," Zoom asked.

I rubbed my hand across my face and replied, "No, Zoom, I am not alright. Esha has done so much damage, I can honestly say that I am uneasy to see what all she has been up to. I have a feeling that even when I kill her, things won't just return to normal. It's no telling how many people she has corrupted with her lies and pussy. Esha would fuck the whole world at once if it meant she got to control everything and everyone around her," I replied.

"Well, she has definitely done that and a whole lot more. I just wish that—"

Before I could finish, Zoom slammed on the brakes. There were some screams in the back, and I bumped my head against the window.

"Is everyone alright?" I asked.

"Yes, we are okay back here. What happened?" Lamont asked.

I looked over at Zoom, and he replied and pointed, "We have visitors."

Looking out the windshield, I saw Esha, Jade, Angel, and Dantez standing in the street, staring at the car. I knew that as soon as I got close that she would sense me because I no longer had the cloaking spell hiding me. She was still my mate, so I knew it was only a matter of time. Zoom had his phone out and was texting someone. He stopped and looked over at Lamont.

"Stay in and watch the girls. King Zaire, I texted Zontae and Nichelle to get some backup here. I am not sure what Esha has up her sleeve, and I know that we can handle it, but we have the girls with us," Zoom stated.

I nodded my head in agreement and replied, "Let's see what the fuck she wants."

"Please be careful, you two. I don't like this at all," Ever stated.

Zoom placed a kiss on her lips and nodded as he opened the car door. I opened my car door as well. He came to my side slightly in front of me as I walked. He was my unofficial bodyguard for the moment, and he was taking that position seriously.

I looked over at Esha in black jeans that hugged her body with a black bodysuit and boots to match. She had her hair straight down her back, and I couldn't help but admire her beauty that was all overshadowed by her hateful black heart.

"Well, if it isn't my loving mate. Did you come to welcome your man home?" I asked sarcastically, stopping about ten feet in front of her.

Her eyes glowed green, and I smiled, knowing that I had pissed her off.

"You tricked me! I thought that I had killed you, and instead, here you are. How did you know what I was planning to do? Whose head did I cut off?" she questioned.

Smiling, I replied, "Well, you see, wifey, I left you over twenty years ago when I walked in on you being fucked in every hole by my best friends, Dantez, Luke, and some shifter. You had other niggas cum running all over and in you, with your nasty ass! Damn septic tank ass pussy for fuck niggas' cum!"

Dantez growled and ran toward me. I growled, and my fangs and claws dropped, preparing for his attack. Dantez spread his huge Seraphim wings and flew above our heads, getting ready to strike. He was about to dive, when his wings burst into flames, and he fell to the ground screaming.

"You bitch!" Esha yelled with her eyes glowing and fangs descending.

I looked over to where her anger was drawn, and a beautiful young woman with braids was standing there with red glowing eyes. She was dressed casually in a long maxi dress, smiling.

"Hey, mama in law! You didn't invite me to the party," she said with a smile.

Zoom mumbled beside me. "Aw hell. Zontae is going to whoop her ass and mine if anything happens to her. That's your daughter-in-law, Zontae's wife, Samara. She is Nichelle's daughter. Let me see if I can get her over here so I can shield all of us."

My heart skipped a beat when he said Nichelle's name. She was the love of my life and should have been my mate. Instead, I got the devil's hoe.

Zoom called Samara over, and she flashed to us. When she got closer, I caught her scent and smelled succubus blood in her system along with something else. I toned down my sense of smell, because she was emitting a pheromone that would draw men in, and I wasn't trying to go there with my son's wife.

"Zoom, they have an army of Seraphim and angels about a mile back. My brother Monroe is watching them now to see if they will move over here. But it must be a setup. I am not sure if they are here to kill you or capture you, so we need to be prepared for anything," Samara whispered low enough for only us to hear.

Zoom's eyes turned white, and I could feel his power moving from his body, covering us and the car with a bluish shield.

Dantez was standing up, and his burnt wings began smoking as he stared a hole into Samara.

"Samara Duvall, I hope you enjoyed your life because I plan to end it for you today! Too bad I didn't get to sample that pussy that had Zontae turn his back on his own mother and Dane turn on his father. How many men have been in that tight little pussy of yours?" Dantez said with an evil grin.

Before he could say anything else, I had flashed over and ripped his spine from his body and tore his head off and threw it at Esha. There was no way in hell that I was going to let him talk to my daughter like that. I felt a sting and noticed he must have gotten a slice in with his claws to my side.

All hell broke loose, and Seraphim appeared and surrounded me. I guess they felt their king being killed. Unfortunately, his ass would regenerate in a day or two because I didn't kill him with a blessed weapon. Zoom dropped the shield and made two magic machetes in his hands. He started slicing through Seraphim as I started stabbing them with my claws and ripping them apart. Samara was fighting them too with fireballs in her hands. I saw Esha heading toward Samara, and I was trying to get to her before she did. Angel was fighting with Lamont, trying to get into the car where Ever and Christy were. I could hear Christy screaming as a Seraph was trying to pull her through the window.

I saw Samara levitate off the ground and raise hair hands in the air. Her nose was bleeding, and the ground started shaking as large fireballs started falling from the sky onto the Seraphim army. They were screaming in pain as the fireballs crashed into them, setting them ablaze.

"Zoom, get everyone in the car!" Samara yelled.

Esha was still running, and I then realized that she was never after Samara. She was trying to get to the car that had Ever and Christy in it. Zoom and I must have noticed at the same time because we flashed toward the car just as the Seraph grabbed Christy, trying to lift her up in the air.

"Let go of my sister!" Ever yelled as she grabbed onto Christy's legs, trying to pull her back in the car. Before we could get to them, Esha pulled Ever to her and pointed a long sharp claw at her throat, pressing in, drawing blood.

"Enough! I will rip her throat out if you don't stop, Samara!" Esha yelled.

"If you hurt her, I swear I will rip your fangs out and slice your throat with them!" Zoom growled with snow white eyes.

Esha smiled, and more blood came from the cut in Ever's neck.

"I suggest you reign in that white magic of yours before you end up in the same place your father is! Samara, I won't repeat myself again!" Esha yelled.

Samara floated down and landed unsteadily beside me. She looked pale, and her nose was pouring blood. I pulled her behind me, keeping one hand on her in case she started to fall.

"So, you would kill your own daughter? I guess I shouldn't be surprised since you left us to fend for ourselves when we were kids!" Ever yelled.

Something flashed across Esha's face, and she smelled Ever's neck. A look of anger twisted her face.

"Ever! Why are you here, and why do you smell different? Did you let someone mate with you!" Esha yelled in Ever's ear.

"She's my mate now, after your minion almost killed her at the hospital! But why the fuck do you care? It's not like you cared before," Zoom replied.

Esha reached down and put her hand on Ever's stomach and screamed, "She's pregnant!"

Zoom and Ever both looked shocked, but I wasn't surprised because I was sleeping in the room next to them last night and heard them consummating their mating bond. I just didn't understand why Esha was so upset about it.

Esha's eyes changed to a dark green that I had never seen before. They were almost black. The skies started to darken, and the wind blew violently around us. Then, Esha's eyes went completely black, and a deep menacing voice came from her mouth.

"You ruined her! She was mine and perfect! Now she has that thing in her belly that ruins every fucking thing I had planned! You will all die for plotting against me!" Esha growled.

Esha sliced Ever across her throat and blood started pouring out. Christy and Zoom screamed. Esha turned her attention to Christy with an evil grin.

"Take her back to my house!" she screamed to the Seraph that held her. He shot into the air with a screaming Christy.

Zoom had Ever cradled in his arms as he poured his blood into her mouth. I flashed over to Esha and grabbed her by the throat and started choking the shit out of her. It was time for her to die, and I was more than happy to be the one to end her life. She had fucked over my sons, my life, and my kingdom. Hell, all she did was fuck; it was the only damn thing she was good at!

I smiled as I watched her struggle to breath and the color leave her skin. Her reign of terror was almost over.

"Die, you treacherous bitch! I hope the Dark One tortures your ass for eternity, you sick ass hoe!" I yelled as the last bit of life left her face. I reached in and snatched the heart out of her chest, tossing it on her lifeless body, wiping the blood off on my jeans.

Samara walked over to me and looked down at Esha and spit on her.

"Good riddance, bitch. Well, King Zaire, I am happy you are alive. I just hate that she ruined your homecoming. But then again, her death has to be the best gift ever," Samara stated with a smile.

I smiled back and walked over to Zoom and Lamont who were helping Ever up. I looked around at the Seraphim body parts that were slowly creeping together. We needed to get out of here soon before they completely regenerated since we didn't have any blessed weapons to fully kill them.

Samara's phone rang, and she stepped away to speak to whoever it was. Ever was crying, and I felt like shit that I couldn't stop her sister from being taken away.

"Okay, that was my brother Monroe. He is following the Seraph that has your sister, and he will get her back. I know that you are afraid for her, but we have to have faith that he will return with her soon. If he's not back by tonight, I will go back out with you and look for her. Sisters are too precious to lose," Samara said, rubbing Ever's arm.

Ever looked at Samara and replied in a shaky tearful voice, "I will give him an hour to bring her back. After that, I am searching for her myself. All we have is each other, and I won't fail her like our mother has."

Zoom replied, "You both have me now, baby. She is my family now too. Let me get you settled with Samara, and I will go out and search for her until I bring her home to you, okay?"

Lamont nodded and said, "That's my niece, and I am going too. Ever, I wasn't there for you both when you were younger, but I plan for making up for that now."

Ever smiled at her uncle and looked into Zoom's eye's and responded, "Can you both go now? I can go with King Zaire and Samara. I just need her back here safe and sound."

I could see the turmoil in Zoom's eyes as he was being torn between staying and protecting his king and his mate or going after his sister-in-law. I decided to make the decision for him.

"Zoom, you and Lamont need to go aid Samara's brother. It's no telling where he is taking her or what problems he might run into while trying to save her. Plus, she needs someone she knows and is comfortable with to bring her back. Samara and I can take care of your mate. Plus, we need to get out of here anyway before these motherfuckers put themselves back together," I stated.

Zoom was in deep thought for a few moments and finally nodded his head in agreement. He kissed Ever deeply on the lips before pulling away.

"Here, take my phone so you can call my brother so he can tell you where he is following the Seraph that took Christy," Samara stated.

"Samara, please take care of my mate and seed. Not to mention yourself, because I am not trying to fight with your crazy ass mate. King Zaire, y'all get the hell out of here as fast as you can. It's no telling what Esha's minions will do when they find out that you killed their queen. Jade and Angel disappeared after Christy was taken. Come on, Lamont. Let's find Christy," Zoom said before flashing away.

"So, you are who Zoom called for backup. I must say I am very impressed by my daughter-in-law, but I would expect nothing less from Nichelle's daughter," I stated.

"Thank you, but I say we get out of here and back to my mom's house before your son gets there. He will not be happy by how much of my powers that I used today," Samara stated while wiping her still bleeding nose.

"Yeah, sounds like him. He always was protective of the ones that he loved. Let's take the car and get out of here. Both of you have bled enough for today," I replied.

"I don't think they have bled enough," a deep voice said from behind me.

I turned toward it and was impaled in the chest by a metal rod and fell to my knees.

"Ever, get in the car! How in the hell are you alive?" Samara yelled.

I looked up, and Esha stood in front of me with her heart in her hand smiling with an evil grin. She shoved her heart back in her chest and licked her fingers. Her eyes were pure black now, and I sensed something different and more powerful about her. Something wasn't right. I pulled the rod out of my chest and tossed it to the side. My chest and side were burning like hell, and I needed to feed fast.

"Well my dear, Samara. You have yourself to thank for my miraculous recovery. That blood of yours works wonders. You were so busy trying to whoop my ass that you didn't even notice that I took it. Plus, I have a few tricks up my sleeve just for you, Samara," Esha explained.

She lifted her hands, and the wind picked up, and big chunks of ice started falling from the sky. Ever got out just before a huge chunk fell on the car and crushed it.

I flashed over and grabbed Ever, placing my body over hers to protect her and the baby, while turning my head to watch Esha and Samara.

Esha looked possessed with her black eyes and hair all over her head. There was a hole in her chest where you could see the blood pumping through her heart. Vampires were not supposed to come back to life when you yanked their hearts out.

Esha raised her hands, and the shower of ice chunks started coming down harder. It was stripping pieces of skin off my back with every strike. Ever was protected but not enough as the chunks got bigger and started cutting her arms.

Samara's eyes turned red with yellow flames in them, and she raised her arms and fire shot out of the ground. It curved and formed a fire wall above and around me and Ever, protecting us from the ice chunks and melting them as soon as they came down.

"Bitch!" Esha yelled in that creepy deep ass voice and flashed, trying to get through the fire wall but not being able to.

Samara increased the flames out of the ground as blood poured from her nose and mouth. I didn't know how much longer she could hold on because she was swaying at the moment.

"Stay down!" I yelled at Ever, and she nodded in agreement.

I picked up the rod that was in my chest earlier and threw it through Esha's stomach. She screamed and yelled with black blood pouring from her mouth. "It's not over! Soon, you will all bow at my feet before I end your lives!"

She flashed away, and the firewall came down.

"Ever, you good?" I asked.

Ever replied, "I'm okay, but Samara doesn't look well."

I turned to Samara just in time to watch her eyes roll back in her head and her body drop. Ever and I both ran over to her, and I lifted her into my arms, and she opened her eyes for a brief moment and whispered an address. I put her in the back seat with Ever climbing beside her to take care of her and took off. I didn't know what the hell just happened, but I had a bad feeling that killing Esha wouldn't be as easy as I thought.

SELENE (LENE)

*S*amara, Nichelle, and I were sitting in the nursery getting to know Monroe, when Samara got a call from Zoom telling her that Esha was about to attack him and King Zaire with her minions. We were all shocked that King Zaire was alive and well. I wondered how Mesa would take the news once he found out. So much was going on, and I was ready to get back to some semblance of normal.

We were stretched thin and had to be smart in how we moved since there was literally chaos all over the Underworld, so I decided to stay here with the babies, and Samara and Monroe went to help Zoom. Omega and Alpha went to take Syren to the Demon realm to prepare her for her awakening, whatever that was. Our mother, Nichelle, was taking care of our father, Santonio, who was still not feeling well, which had me worried. It was so much happening to our family that had me on edge.

I had baby Zaire in my arms because he was the only one that was awake and hungry. Zaniyah and Mena were knocked out, cuddled up next to each other. I looked down into his now hazel eyes and smiled. He was going to have his mother and I chasing all the thots away. I couldn't wait to have a son and playmate for Zaire. After what happened between Mesa and I in the sauna, I just knew that we had created a mini version of my husband.

I was about to get up and walk with Zai when my head started swimming and I got nauseous. I quickly placed Zai down in the bassinet that was beside the chair and sat back, closing my eyes as the visions took over, flashing through my mind.

I saw a vision of me rocking a baby that was wrapped in a blue blanket. I smiled and pressed a hand to my stomach knowing that our son was growing inside of me. Then the visions changed and turned dark. I was standing in a cemetery in front of a grave with my daughter's name on it. Beside it was Zaniyah and baby Zaire's grave. In the background, I heard laughter coming from the mist. The figure was shrouded in the mist, and I was trying to make out who it was.

The figure grew closer, and Jazz's face came into view, and she was covered in blood.

"I am coming for your little bastards, and you will be burying them real soon. Mesa was mine, and you took him away from me! I won't let you and those brats take away my father too!" Jazz said with an evil glare.

I heard the cries of our precious babies from the ground as Jazz laughed. I was digging up the graves but couldn't get to them or find them. My eyes popped open, and Zai had my finger in his hand and was staring at me with dark brown eyes that were almost black; not his normal hazel. I felt warmth flowing into me that calmed me down from my vision. With my free hand, I wiped the tears from my face and pried my finger from Zai. His eyes changed back to hazel, and he started playing with his feet. How did he calm me down and bring me out of my visions? He wasn't supposed to be able to use his magic until puberty.

I was worried about the girls, so I picked up Zai and headed to the nursery to check on the girls. When I got there, both girls were still sleeping peacefully, cuddled up to each other. I placed Zai in the crib beside them, and he started playing with Mena's hair. I smiled because he loved his cousin and sister. I knew that he would protect them from any harm.

I heard the door open, and my mother walked in and of course went straight to the crib to fawn over her grandbabies. I smiled as she kissed each one of them and started playing with Zai's feet, which was something he loved for people to do. I was about to ask about Santonio, when an overwhelming feeling of danger hit me. I bent over and grabbed my stomach, trying to calm down the pain and dread that was flowing through it.

Nichelle grabbed me and helped me into one of the rockers that was in the room.

"Lene, are you okay?" Nichelle asked.

I shook my head 'no' and replied, "No, Mom. Something isn't right. I had a vision a little while ago, and now I have this overwhelming sense of danger, and it feels like it is getting closer."

I told her about the vision, and she stared off in deep thought. She got up and ran out of the room. I frowned, trying to figure out why the hell did she leave out of the room. She ran back in and made a circle in the middle of the floor and sat in the center.

"Selene, come sit with me and don't say a word," Nichelle stated.

I sat down in front of her, and she grabbed my hands and sat with her eyes closed. Her hands started heating up, and I started pulling my hands away because it started to burn. Nichelle's grip grew stronger, and her eyes snapped open, and they were a pure pearl color with a milky rainbow of colors swimming in them.

She stared at me and shook her head 'no' and said in a different otherworldly voice, "Selene, do not break the connection between you and your mother. It is imperative that she completes this spell. Lives depend on it, especially the Duvall children."

I looked at her and replied, "Who are you?"

She smiled as a red and white light glowed all around her, framing her silhouette and responded, "I am your grandmother, Nahla, the original Red Queen. Your mother has summoned me because the time has come to fulfill the destiny that was foretold centuries ago. A great evil has been unleashed onto the earth, and our family was chosen to be the protectors of the human race and the Underworld. The darkness has finally revealed itself, and it has started to spread like a cancer; it must be stopped before it can do any more damage than it already has."

I sat there with my mouth open, taking in everything that she was saying. The feeling of evil kept pressing down on my chest like a fifty-pound weight. I was trying to come up with the right words to say to the spirit of my grandmother speaking through my mother.

I had finally gathered my thoughts and asked, "How do we stop it and protect the children?"

"All will be revealed soon. There will be someone coming soon that will help you and your siblings understand your destiny and what you need to do to fulfill it. You must keep an open-mind because sometimes the ones that we view as enemies could be your only hope. Your mother and I will strengthen you all with our combined powers. Just let your mother do what she needs to do, and don't defy her. Have faith, dear child, as I have faith in all of you," Nahla said with a smile.

Her eyes closed, and then I heard the perfect blend of Nahla and Nichelle's voices chanting. My hands felt like they were on fire, but this time I took the pain. Nothing was stopping me from doing whatever I had to do to protect Zaniyah, Zaire, and Mena.

Nichelle opened her eyes, and this time they were red and sparkling with facets like a ruby. She opened her mouth, and the most melodic voice started chanting, and it felt like the words were wrapping around my body and soul and soothing every fear, pain, and anxiety that had been there before.

"*Spiritus invoco mearum tutelam beati liberorum ponat corona. De illis nunc in hoc planum est quod defendat malum. Super filios nostros confero belli venturum. Magicae album quod in iis vehementer destruendo malos Multis minatur vobis munera all. Thank occidere!*" Nichelle's voice echoed in my head in Latin.

"Spirits of my ancestors, I call upon you to place a ring of protection over these blessed children. Protect them from the evil that is present on this plane. I transfer my powers over to my children for the battle that is to come. Strengthen them with the white magic that will aid them in destroying the evil that threatens to kill us all. Thank you for your many blessings and gifts!" Her voice boomed throughout the room.

My body started feeling heavy as the red glow moved from Nichelle, over my body, and some moved over the babies and out through the window. The same burning that I felt in my hands was now making its way through my body. I gritted my teeth and closed my eyes against the pain until a cool sensation eased the burn. I opened my eyes slowly and looked at my mother laid out on the floor.

I crawled over to her and tried to shake her awake, but she wasn't budging. I checked her pulse, and it was strong along with her breathing. I released the breath I was holding in relief. I slowly stood up and checked on the babies in the crib, and they were all awake and staring at me. It was a little eerie the way they were all focused on me as if they were trying to tell me something. I noticed a red glow in their little cheeks, and I wondered if any of the magic was affecting them. All three then closed their eyes together and went to sleep.

I covered them up and placed a kiss on each one of them. I placed a pillow under Nichelle's head and a cover over her body.

"*Hide, watch, and wait; she is coming,*" a voice whispered in my mind.

I shivered and pulled my mother behind the sofa and covered her up. I went into the closet which had shutters on the door so I could see out with a good view of the babies. I watched and waited for what seemed like forever, but it was in fact only about fifteen minutes. There was a nervous energy running through my body as the window opened by itself. I watched as Jazz slithered into the window like the snake that she was. I instantly felt my body growing hot with anger knowing that she was here to hurt our children. I watched as she peeped around the room to make sure no one was there. The protection around the house most likely was down because Nichelle was passed out from using up her magic on that spell.

She smiled as she walked over to the crib and peeked in.

"Well, little man, it looks like you are the only one awake. Don't worry, I won't hurt you. I will take you to my father and let him suck the life out of your little yellow ass! Then you can join your sister and cousin in death. I plan to kill them before we leave. Too bad your mommy and auntie are such bitches! Don't worry; my sister and I will be there to console your daddies," Jazz stated.

Zai must have woken up when she entered the room. Jazz was about to bend over into the crib when I started easing out of the closet so I could get to her before she got to the babies. But, before I had the door open, she grabbed her throat and started choking. She was staring down into the crib in shock. I ran out of the closet and punched her ass in the face while she was choking, to knock her away from the crib. She fell back, gasping for air on the floor.

"Dumb ass bitch!" I yelled as I kicked her in the mouth, and one of her fangs flew out of her mouth. I peeked in the crib, and Zai's eyes were black again, and he had a frown on his face. I rubbed a hand on his cheek, and they changed to the normal hazel color. I needed to talk to Zontae and Samara, because Zai was using magic that he shouldn't have at this age. What had the Forbidden Book done to my nephew?

Jazz moaned, drawing my attention to her, and I kicked her in the side, and she screamed. I grabbed her by the hair and dragged her out of the room and into the guest room that was next door. I didn't want the kids to see any more violence if they didn't have to, especially Zai. She was screeching, and it was getting on my nerves, so I used my telepathy and made her shut the hell up! I had discovered I could do it while I was training a few days ago. Who knew it would come in handy so quickly.

Once we were in the room, I pulled her cell phone out of her pocket and tossed it on the bed. I started stomping her ass and watched as the silent tears and snot streamed down her face. I made sure I pulled the baby monitor out of my pocket so I could watch the babies while I beat her ass.

After kicking her a few more times, I unsealed her mouth because I had questions and I needed answers. Plus, my head was starting to hurt from using a power that I was just now learning. I wiped the blood away that had trickled down my face from my nose.

I pulled Jazz up by her hair and slammed her down into the chair and asked, "Where is Luke hiding out, hoe?"

She tried to spit in my face, but I stopped it mid-air with my mind and made it hit her back in the face. She wiped it off and glared at me. I bet her ditzy ass wouldn't spit at me again.

"Fuck you, Selene! I am not telling you shit! Once my father finds out that you have me here, he's going to come and rescue me and kill all of you and your ugly ass kids!" Jazz screamed.

I smiled as I played her words over in my head. I had the perfect way to bring Luke out of hiding.

"Well, well, well, who knew that you could come up with an idea that didn't have to do with taking dick in every hole. You know that you were dumb for coming back here, right? I mean, you had to know that we would be watching the kids carefully, so I think you had to be desperate to come here. So, what's really going on?" I questioned.

She had a stunned, guilty look on her face and then tried to hide it, but it was too late. I concentrated on her mind and paralyzed her. I felt something surge in me that I had never felt before. My telepathy took on a new direction and led me to go closer into her mind. I could hear her thoughts and see her memories playing through my mind like a movie. I saw the confrontation between her and her father and the plans she had for the babies. She was going to bring Zai to her father to suck dry and smother Zaniyah and Mena. My blood boiled as I felt her happiness at the thoughts of killing them and hurting our family.

I felt the anger rise, and I applied more pressure to her head. I tried to stop myself, but then I said fuck her and kept squeezing her brain as she pissed and shit herself, but I still wasn't satisfied. I applied pressure to her organs and watched as blood poured out of her orifices. She was screaming, and my head was banging, but I wasn't stopping until this bitch was dead. She had caused too much pain to live, and she was trying to kill our babies. She was now whimpering, and I smiled as I tasted my blood in my mouth from overusing my powers.

"You fucked with the wrong family, Jazz! Die painfully, you empty-headed, skeezy hoe!" I said as the light started dying from her eyes.

I saw her heart in my mind and moved it through her body,

making her choke until it ripped out of her mouth onto the floor, and her body dropped. I called the firepower that was part of my Phoenix heritage that Nahla just gifted me. It was instinctively now that I could feel my powers so strongly, I knew how to do so, whereas before, they were hidden deep, and I had no clue how to use them.

I used my mind and ripped her head into two pieces and set it and her heart on fire and watched them burn until they were ashes. The only thing left was her body, but I needed it. There was a plastic bin in the corner that I moved toward me and started moving what was left of her into it, using my mind. There was no way I was touching her body.

The door flew open, and Mesa flashed to me with glowing green eyes, followed by Zeus and Zontae. He wrapped his arms around me and kissed my forehead. He wiped the blood from my cheeks and nose with his hands. I closed my eyes because his presence always had a way of calming me down, and right now, I really needed it. Mesa stepped back and looked down at the mess I had created in the bin.

"What happened? I felt your fear, and then you were pissed off like a motherfucker. We got back here as soon as we could. Who is that in the bin?" Mesa asked.

"That would be Jazz. She was coming here to kidnap baby Zai and take him to Luke so he could suck the rest of the Forbidden Book from him. Then she was going to smother Zaniyah and Mena, so the bitch had to die!" I answered with an angry growl.

Mesa stepped back from me, and so did Zeus and Zontae, who were all staring at me strangely.

"Umm, niece, did something else happen to you while we were gone? Your eyes are red with yellow in them," Zeus asked.

I looked in the mirror, and sure enough, it looked like flames were dancing in my eyes. This was strange as hell, because normally, they were brown or green, depending on my mood.

"She has been given the power of our ancestors. She has had a visit from her grandmother, Nahla, my mother, the original Red Queen," my mother said as she came into the room looking tired and pale.

"Mama, are you okay?" I asked.

84

She smiled and nodded her head 'yes' and replied, "Yes, Lene, I am okay. You did well while I was out. I am sorry that I wasn't able to explain everything before the ceremony began, but she wanted to speak to you herself."

"It's okay. I am just glad that you are okay, even if you don't look like it," I responded.

"Damn, Lene. You fucked her ass up! Hell, her ass implants popped out. Zontae, you owe me twenty dollars. I told you her ass was fake! Bitch had more silicone than brains," Mesa stated.

Zontae and Mesa were laughing, and it looked as if they didn't have a care in the world. It made me wonder if Zoom told them about their father or not.

"Mesa, did Zoom get in contact with you?" I asked.

Mesa shook his head 'no' and replied, "He called, but I couldn't hear all that he was saying. The only part I heard was that he was meeting us here. What, did something happen?"

My mama and I looked at each other, and she nodded her head for me to be the one to break the news to them.

Before I could say anything, Zontae doubled over, holding his head.

"Ahh, fuck! Something is wrong with Samara!" he yelled.

"She went to meet up with Zoom. Esha showed up, and Samara and Monroe went to help them," I responded.

Zontae's eyes turned red, and I knew that there was going to be hell to pay. Right now, we needed to find them.

There was a banging on the door downstairs, and we all headed out of the room to see what it was. Mesa pulled me back behind him as Zeus opened the door. None of the men were prepared to see the sight that greeted them.

MESA

*U*ncle Zeus was standing at the door just staring. It made me wonder who in the hell was at the door, so I peeked around him and saw my father who was supposed to be dead, standing there with an unconscious Samara in his arms and another woman with blonde hair.

Zontae snatched Samara from him so fast, I didn't even see him flash over to him. Nichelle walked over and started checking on Samara.

"Is this some type of sick ass joke! Who the fuck are you?" my uncle Zeus asked.

I was wondering the same damn thing because my pops was supposed to be dead. We saw his head in a box and burned his body to ashes, so I wasn't sure what kind of games someone was playing with us.

"Mesa, this is what I was about to tell you. Zoom called and said that he had found your father. That's what he was trying to tell you over the phone," Lene stated.

I stared at the man who was supposed to be my father and called bullshit. There was no way in hell that he could be alive.

"I know that all of you have a lot of questions and doubts with me standing here. I promise that if you hear me out, I can explain why I am standing here alive and not dead," King Zaire stated.

Dana walked in with Mary and Lawrynn and said, "He's telling the truth. We had to switch him with a Morph in order to save everyone's lives and fulfill the destiny that was foretold. Come on; let's have a seat so that we can put everything together because the evil grows by the minute. The longer it is out, the more damage that it does to the world. More for you to clean up."

We all walked into the family room and had a seat. Devin and Dane were already there waiting on us, with Slice watching them to make sure they didn't do any sneaky shit. Hell, I really didn't want them in the house with Lene and Mara, but we needed them at the moment. Plus, they knew we would fuck them up if they even tried anything with our mates.

Nichelle brought the babies downstairs along with Santonio. I looked over at my back from the dead daddy and saw his jaw twitch looking at Santonio and Nichelle interact. I guess he was still carrying a torch for her. More messy shit to come from what I could tell.

Dana and my father explained how he caught Esha hoeing it out with the council and having to hide out in order to protect us and the kingdom. We introduced our evil turned good, I guess, grandmother, and she explained to them about the Forbidden Book and told the same story she told us. This shit was unbelievable on so many levels. My family was well and truly fucked up, and I was tired of shit being revealed about them. It was bad when Zontae and I were the least fucked up in the family.

Samara had come to, and was at the moment, feeding from Zontae's neck as he listened in on everything that was being said. I could tell he was taking everything in and processing. Hell, I was too.

Our father told us about Christy being taken and Esha coming back from the dead, even after he ripped off her head and her heart from her chest. I guess being the fucking Forbidden Book came with benefits.

"Mesa and Zontae, we were coming here to also tell you that Esha had more children that she hid. Christy and Ever are your mother's daughters, which makes them your sisters," Zaire explained.

I looked over at the woman that came in with my father and really looked at her. I didn't know how I missed it when she came in, but she was the spitting image of Esha. Wasn't this some shit!

Ever walked over to me and extended her hand and said, "Hi, I'm Ever, I guess your little sister and Zoom's mate. I want to get to know you and Zontae, believe me, but I am worried about Christy. We need to get her back. She has seizures, and I have her medication. If she gets stressed out, she could have one, and there is no telling what will happen then."

I nodded my head, and Zontae replied, "We got the both of you. I know you don't know us, but I promise you that we won't let anything happen to either one of you. Zoom is one of the best at tracking people down. He will find her; you just have to have faith. Slice, take my sister into one of the guest bedrooms and make sure she is comfortable. Call Zoom and get an update and let her speak with him. Hopefully he has caught up with Monroe by now."

Ever hugged him and then came over and hugged me and replied, "Thank you both. I just need to know that she and Zoom are safe. I will freshen up afterward and come back down to see what I can do to help."

She left, and I looked over at Zontae and shook my head in disbelief and said, "I swear that our family is really fucked up. I don't even know how to feel about having two sisters that Esha hid from us. That's some foul shit for real."

Zontae rubbed Samara's hair and replied, "To be honest with you, bruh, at this point, I am just numb from all the secrets and shit floating around here and blowing up in our faces. No offense, Pops and Grandma Black Witch, but y'all are some lying ass motherfuckers, and I am not sure that I can trust either one of you. I just want you to know that if you are playing some type of game and I find out, I will not hesitate to put you down. Blood or not."

"I don't play games, son. I understand your trust issues because you have went through some fucked up shit these past few weeks. So I will let it slide for now, but watch your tone when you speak to your elders. You are more than welcome to try and put me down, but believe me, that shit won't be easy," Zaire stated.

My pops and Zontae stared each other down, and I just waited for shit to get popping. My ass was going to sit back and watch to make sure my brother whooped his disappearing ass.

Grandma Mary cleared her throat and said, "I think that we all have more important things to worry about right now and that is how to stop the Dark One from taking over. We need to figure out what we are going to do and handle it quickly, and you are right, you shouldn't trust me at all, because my past deeds speak for themselves. Evil has dwelled in my soul for a long time, and to be honest, I am not asking for forgiveness or a relationship with my grandchildren because I will be dead soon. My path was chosen a long time ago, and all I have time for now is to atone for the many sins that I have committed. Now, you can kill me, but then you would be killing the only person here that knows how to kill Esha and the Forbidden Book. I don't think you want to take those chances, Zontae. Now, where should we begin, Luke or Esha?"

Damn, Grandma was gangsta. I guess that's where we got our stubbornness from. Zontae nodded his head toward Pops and Mary, coming to an uneasy but necessary agreement.

"I say we continue with the plan to get to Luke first. I have Jazz's cell phone and can lure him somewhere using it. I went through Jazz's mind and know most of her memories, so I know I can convince him to come. The main thing now is knowing how to kill him and get the book out of him," Lene explained.

"When the fuck did you learn to start reading people's minds and shit?" I asked.

She smiled and replied, "I am not quite sure. After the spell, it just came to me. It was like it awakened powers that I didn't even know I had."

"Wow, Selene. That's a good gift to have. I am impressed. You were always a fast learner anyways," Devin stated, making googly-eyes at my mate.

I looked at this stupid, disrespectful ass motherfucker, sitting here trying to push up on my mate like my ass wasn't sitting here. I picked up the candle beside me and threw it and hit his ass upside the head with it.

"Not today, Green Mile. Keep your eyes off that one before I forget that you might be of some use and send your ass on to glory. Don't end up like your sister upstairs," I threatened.

Dana screamed and took off running upstairs. Zeus followed behind her, and I cursed under my breath. Hell, with everything going on, I forgot that no one had told her about Jazz. I felt bad that she lost her child, but not sorry that that hoe was dead. Hell, Jazz got her wish and would be getting all the dead dick she wanted with her graveyard pussy ass.

"I am with Lene. We need to take care of Luke because battling Esha will require all of our concentration. So how do we kill Luke and the part of the Forbidden Book that is in him?" I asked.

Mary looked over at Lawrynn and said, "Lawrynn is a Kanima. Her venom has the power to weaken Luke's strength. We might need her to get close to Luke, so that she can either bite him or scratch him. Then we can try and kill him. The bad thing is we have to find a way to keep the Forbidden Book piece away before it makes its way back into baby Zaire."

I noticed that Lene tensed up when they mentioned baby Zai. Something was wrong.

"I have to tell you both something, Zontae and Mara. Zai has his powers already and has been using them. He brought me out of my visions and used them on Jazz when she was trying to reach into the crib," Selene explained.

"It's the piece of Forbidden Book in him. We have to hide him in another realm while we kill Luke and Esha. It's the only way we know for sure that the book won't jump into him. Nichelle can take him, and Lawrynn can be their bodyguard while they are away. I promise that she will guard them with her life. I say to the Fae realm with King Kaidan because it is disguised by their magic. As a matter of fact, all of the children should go," Mary stated.

"We will be fine, Mara. I promise. Just make sure that you keep yourself safe, and I will protect my grandbabies," Nichelle said.

Dana was going with them because she was taking Jazz's death hard. Zontae contacted Kaidan, and although there was chaos going on in his realm, but he was more than happy to come and escort them to his home. We just needed to get some things together first and get ready to say goodbye to our children. Plus, we needed to get Christy back so she could go with them. Nichelle started gathering everything we needed to trap and kill Luke. I just hoped that everything went according to plan, because the fate of the world and our children was now in our hands.

ESHA

*a*s soon as I got back to my safe house, I started taking a shower to wash all of the blood off my body. My chest still hurt from where Zaire ripped my heart out. If it hadn't been for Samara's blood, I wouldn't be alive right now. I can't believe that he had fooled me all of these years with a Morph. He had me fucking a complete stranger like some hoe off the streets. I choose who I give this good stuff to. If you couldn't increase my money or power, you wouldn't get it.

I felt different now after coming back from the dead. More alive and powerful somehow. The only problem I had was that I was hearing voices speaking to me, telling me to do things. I had always heard him for as long as I could remember, but it was usually a suggestion or two. Now he was demanding for me to do things. I always listened, so I didn't know why he was so upset.

I got dressed and walked into the room that held my youngest daughter, Christy. She was asleep on the bed from the potion that I gave her earlier, because her screams were working my nerves. I sat down in the chair beside the bed and pushed a strand of her red-streaked blonde hair out of her face. She was beautiful just like she and her sister were created to be. Too bad her sister was ruined, and I couldn't use her anymore.

Jade walked in and sat down in the chair by the window and looked at Christy, shaking her head. I knew that she would come to me eventually with questions about my daughters. Jade was smart, and I had to be careful how I handled her. I had plans for her also, so I had to tread lightly.

"You can stop staring at her and go ahead and ask me what you want to ask me, Jade. I know you have a lot of questions," I stated.

Jade pointed at Christy and replied, "So, you have daughters that no one knew about. Why didn't you bring them to the Underworld? I must admit I feel some type of way because you go around calling me your daughter when you already had two that you have been hiding, and I want to know why."

I knew that she would be jealous because that's just how Jade was. I knew I had to tell her most of the truth but hide the part that was vital to my plans. No one would know about those but the voice inside of me. He was my one true confidant when I needed him. I just tolerated everyone else and used them to my advantage. To be honest with you, everyone was beneath me, and soon they would all bow down and do as they were told. The voice in my head chuckled in agreement.

"You know how I feel about humans and finding ways to use them to do everything that I tell them to do. Well years ago, I met Daniel, who was a biochemist. He was looking for a cure for sickle cell anemia because his brother, Lamont, was suffering with it. I faked being an assistant to get my hands on a serum he had that would mutate cells. I needed it to create the perfect blend between my genes and human genes without changing that person into a vampire. The problem was, Daniel was very tight lipped about his creations. I ended up making him fall in love with me, and those lips started to loosen. I ended up turning his brother and making Daniel think that he had cured Lamont," I explained.

Jade looked confused and replied, "Wait a minute. It takes years to get approval to do clinical trials. How did he give the serum to his brother without getting in trouble?"

I smiled and replied, "It's amazing what money and pussy can do. Imagine when you have a lot of both. I had a lab in the basement that I worked in and did experiments on humans that didn't have any family that would miss them. The serum would always make the humans bloodthirsty, and that is not what I wanted. I needed the perfect blend of immortal and human to create an army that obeyed only me. I was becoming frustrated with all my failures and was about to give up and kill all of my subjects and Daniel. Then one day, Daniel started talking about changing the genetic cells before the person was born, while they were still in the uterus. I fucked him and only him real good for the next few nights without a condom. All the while I was injecting myself with the serum so it could be in my system when the baby was created. A week later, I found out I was pregnant."

"Where was King Zaire during all of this, and how did you get away with being pregnant twice and no one noticing your swollen belly?" Jade questioned.

"Zaire was with Zeus, and they were in mourning in the Demon realm for their sister Ari, Slice's mother. She conveniently bled out and died during childbirth after having Slice. Mourning in the Demon realm is for thirty days, so I had Ever, and when I was pregnant with Christy, their father was killed by an assassin. So, I was free to do what I needed to do and cover it up," I responded.

"Wow. You are something else, Esha. You killed Zaire's sister and father just to hide your secrets. That's some scandalous shit right there, for real. I mean, I just assumed that their deaths were not a coincidence, but now to hear that you were responsible, blows my mind. I guess the other big question is, what are your daughters, and what did you mean by Ever isn't perfect?" Jade asked.

Before I could answer, the door flew open, and Cas came stomping in with a mean look on her face.

"You lying bitch! I went to the address that you gave me for the B-packs, and that shit was burned the fuck down! I told you not to fuck with me, but it seems that you didn't get the memo! I had a lot of money tied up in this, and I made a lot of promises for deliveries. Where is my shit, Esha!" Cas yelled.

I closed my eyes to push the anger down that I was feeling. Someone had burned down my warehouse with not only the B-Packs, but the tainted flu shots and my cell serum was in there. It had to be Zontae and Mesa that did this to me. They ruined my greatest masterpieces. Why was everything falling apart just when everything was starting to fall into place. The voice in my head soothed me with his power and love. I felt energized when he caressed me from within my body. My silent lover, confidant, and friend.

"Crazy bitch, did you hear me! I don't know what the fuck is going on in your crazy ass head, spacing out and shit, but you need to put those green ass eyes on me and tell me what the hell is going on," Cas stated.

I sneered at her and replied, "First of all, little girl, watch how you talk to your elders. I will rip your throat out. Now I had no clue that the warehouse had burned down. I had more important things to worry about than watching a pile of bricks. You think you are the only one that lost something? I lost more than you will ever know, so I suggest you find out who did it and make them pay."

Cas rolled her eyes and crossed her arms to her chest and responded, "Fuck you, Esha! Ever since I got into it with you, it has been some shit. You might scare those pigeon head hoes over there, but you don't put any fear in my heart. I want my money and product now, or there will be hell to pay. Don't you think you have enough people after you right now? I don't think you want to make an enemy of me."

I was about to kill her, but his voice caressed me and whispered in my head, *"Let her live and give her what she wants for now. We need the money, and once we have it, we can kill her and take over her territory and her workers. Be patient, my love. We need to start the final phase of our plan tonight. We don't have time for this nonsense."*

I calmed down and took a deep breath, thinking about how to

rectify the situation without killing this bitch. It came to me in an instant, and I smiled.

"I don't have the product, but I know where there is a big stash of it. The Dynasty Boyz have a warehouse where they keep a backup supply if something happens to the main one. It doesn't have any of the tainted B-Packs, but it does have the high-quality packs that Zontae has personally made. I am sure that there is also plenty of money there. I will even drop my percentage down to 30 percent instead of 50 percent as a sign of good faith. Once your uncle comes back, he can mix up the potion for the tainted B-Packs and have the whole Underworld hooked," I stated.

"I actually know the potion myself and can help with making the B-Packs potent and addictive. Us pigeon head hoes are good for something besides spreading our legs, right, cuz?" Jade said sarcastically.

Cas rolled her eyes and shrugged her shoulders and replied, "Fine. But if I don't find shit, I promise you that you won't like me being your enemy. Now, give me the address so I can get out of here."

I gave her the address, and she stomped out of the room.

Jade shook her head and stated, "You know that she is going to be a problem, right? My cousin is getting impatient because she hasn't seen any money yet. Not to mention, she will snitch and tell Zontae about this safe house if she doesn't get what she wants. She is a spoiled brat and has always gotten her way."

I scoffed and waved her off. Cas was beneath me, and soon she wouldn't be a problem at all. Either the Dynasty Boyz or Zontae would kill her before I even had a chance to blink. If she made it out of there alive, then I would kill her once I got her customer list. Either way, I was winning.

"It will all work out. Don't worry about it, Jade. We have more important matters to attend to. Have you seen Angel? I need him to take care of some things for me," I said while side-eyeing Jade. She thought that I didn't know that they had been fucking each other all week.

"Umm, I think that he was gathering the herbs that you needed for the ceremony you wanted to have. You never did tell me what the ceremony was about. Did you need me to prepare anything?" Jade replied.

I stared at her lying ass for a moment. She was just fucking him before she came in because I could smell his scent all over her. I guess she liked the taste of my pussy; he was just eating it as soon as I got in because I was stressed out from dying and coming back to life. But hey, if she liked it, I loved it. Plus, their little situationship would help me out with the final plan.

"You know what, Jade? I do need you to get everything prepared in the living room. We can have a small reception before the ceremony to boost morale after the fight with Samara and Zaire. I will prepare Christy while you get everything ready in the small room beside the living room. Make sure that it's marked private. I need my special black candles in there, and make sure that the couch is draped in the spare satin sheets that I keep for my bed," I explained.

Jade scrunched up her nose and replied, "Are you sure you want to use those candles? They smell like death."

I chuckled because the wax was made with the ashes from corpses, but she didn't need to know that. She just needed to obey me.

"Just light them and get everything prepared. Oh, I forgot, tell everyone to wear silk black pajama bottoms for the men and black silk nightgowns for the women. Make sure that there is plenty of alcohol available and no lights, just candles. Find Angel and Dantez and send them up. I need to speak with them about some things," I replied.

"Oh, you never finished telling me what happened between their father and you. Not to mention, what are they since they are half vampire?" Jade questioned.

I was hoping that her curiosity had been satisfied, but I guess not.

"My daughters were planned and created by me to take over my legacy. They will never be fully vampire because of the serum that their father created. Ever has no clue of the hardships and gifts that she will face since Zoom decided to save her and mate with her. I am not sure of her outcome because I never planned for her to mate with an Underworlder. Luckily, Christy hasn't been touched by an Underworlder, so her body will receive the spell that I need to perform. We also need to siphon her blood; it has special properties that I don't want to fall into the wrong hands. It would ruin my plans, and I have come too far to have them stopped now. Daniel caught me giving the girls the serum and threatened to destroy the serum and the formula. I couldn't have that, so he had a little accident at the lab. It gave me the perfect opportunity to make it look like the serum and all of his notes were destroyed in the fire, but in actuality, I had them both and have been using them to create my own personal army of enhanced humans," I explained.

"I thought you said that they were too blood thirsty to do you any good, and where are you keeping them?" Jade asked.

"I realized that I could use them to attack the humans and make trouble for Zontae and the vampires. I am going to release them on the humans, and the hunters will believe it's the vampires going rogue and letting their bloodlust take over. The way that they eat, they should be able to kill hundreds a week and get rid of the trash ass humans. Their bites will make the humans deathly sick, and then some will die; others will turn into a Dreg. So, it's a win-win situation," I explained.

Jade smiled and replied, "I like that. Taking a mistake and turning into something fabulous. Now I understand why you needed the basement at the hospital. But I didn't see a lot of them there; maybe about twenty of them in the cells."

"Yes, those are actually my throwaways. The ones that are the most dangerous are able to blend in with normal humans. I released them yesterday into the city to start my ultimate plan of domination," I answered with a smile.

"So what are we doing with Christy then?" Jade asked.

I didn't notice my voice changing to a deep soul shaking timbre, until I saw the frightened look on Jade's face. It was too late, and when he wanted to speak, he spoke. He didn't usually speak to anyone but me. But recently, he was talking more, especially when he was mad or he was about to kill someone. It felt strange to feel him taking over, but he was mine, and I was his, so I knew he wouldn't do anything to hurt me.

"My next step is to ensure that my legacy will live on. That is what the ceremony is about. When I had Zontae and Mesa, I just knew that my sons would rule and take over the world. Instead, I got pussies that wanted to be just like their father and treat everyone as equals, which they are not. Unfortunately, when I had Christy, I was told I could not bear any more children. I need a male heir that can carry on my work in taking over this world. Ever was supposed to be my personal vessel to carry my heir and pass on the cell gene into him to make him more powerful than any Underworlder on this planet. But she is ruined because she is carrying Zoom's baby. Christy, however, is a good candidate to take her place. I am very meticulous in my planning and have a reason for everything I do. Even now, I have a backup plan for my backup plans. Although my backup plan isn't top choice, it will do. I should have brought the girls here with me, but they would have ruined my plans. Nichelle popped up with more kids, and I needed to handle that. When I went in search of them, my daughters were gone from the projects that I had left them in. Stupid bitches got thrown out! Daughters are worthless, unless they can open their legs and help advance your position. Sons are where your power lies," he stated.

Jade stared for a moment with a frightened look on her face. She backed away toward the door and left. My love was laughing as she left.

"Why did you have to scare her away?" I asked as I looked in the mirror.

My lover replied, "She is worthless and beneath you, Esha. There are only a few reasons that I have allowed you to keep her around. Before the ceremony, you need to do the temporary possession spell that I taught you. It's very important for the ceremony tonight. Luckily, tonight is a full moon; the ceremony should produce the heir that I need. Now, we need to rest. Let's go to bed before everyone gets here."

I nodded my head 'yes,' and I ran a finger through Christy's hair before we left, and admired her beauty. I could tell my lover was excited for the ceremony, and I was fine with giving him my daughter. We all make sacrifices for the ones that we love, and Christy was my gift to him. Once the child was born, then she would be put into a deep sleep in case he wanted more children. If he didn't, then we could just slit her throat and move on to raise our new children.

MONROE

J unfolded myself from the window where I was camouflaged. They had Christy as they called her in a room for the better part of an hour. This was the first time that they had left her alone, and I needed to get her the fuck out of here before Esha and her delusional ass did some freaky shit to her. Who the hell talks about fucking their own daughter? Bitch in here talking to herself like she had a freaking split personality and shit. You had to watch those crazy ones.

I crept over to Christy who was still knocked out. It didn't look like she weighed much, so I figured I could fly her down and be gone before anyone realized what was going on. That however changed when Dantez stepped into the room and saw me.

"Well, if it isn't Nichelle's long-lost son. It's a shame that Dana hid you before I could get to you and kill you. I mean, your daddy was whining and moaning like a little bitch begging for me not to kill you and kill him instead. I mean that shit took all the fun out of killing him. I wanted him to fight back or run, but he just sat there and let me cut his head off. But the good thing is, I get the chance to kill you this time, and your ass won't escape. Plus, your sister took my life earlier, and I would love to pay her back by killing someone that she loves.

Then I need to pay her fine ass a visit, hell, Selene too. Maybe I can have a sister sandwich on my dick," he said as he locked the door.

I smiled, looking at Dantez because he was one of the reasons why I came out of hiding. My father, from what I heard, was a good man, and he took him away from me. So I was about to get my revenge and save the girl. Cool. I could play the hero and executioner all in one.

"You can try and kill me, motherfucker. I would like to see you try it. I have been waiting to get at your ass for a long time, and look at the blessing that I have in front of me. I am going to make you suffer for killing and even thinking about my sisters. You want my life? You come and try and take it," I responded with a smile because he had no clue what he was getting in to.

Dantez spread his wings out, and his eyes turned white, letting me know that he was about to attack. I needed to end this quickly before anyone else in the building came by to check on Christy.

I smiled, and my eyes changed to their supernatural color, and I watched Dantez stare in shock as my form started to develop. He tried to take off running, but it was too late. With my claw, I snatched him before he could get to the door and pulled him toward my jaws. I punctured his skin, filling him with my venom to keep him quiet. Then I burned the flesh off his face and watched it slide off to the bone. My powers were blessed, so he wouldn't be coming back from this. I crunched down on his skull and broke it into pieces. His body dropped to the ground, and I ripped out his heart and set it on fire and watched that motherfucker burn until it was ashes. I scooped them up and blew them out the window. I placed a hidden roving eye that I got from a sorcerer that made them for me, under the windowsill. In case Esha moved safe houses, it would follow her and send the videos back to me. Got to love supernatural technology. Before I came out of hiding, I was a bounty hunter that specialized in finding the worst of the worst in the Underworld. I went by Haze, and I always reported to one person, so no one really knew my face.

Boom! Boom! Boom!

Someone was banging on the door. I grabbed Christy and flashed to the balcony. My wings spread out behind me casting large shadows on the wall. I leapt off the balcony, and the air caught under my wings, and I started soaring across the sky. I checked on Christy, and she snuggled into my chest as her blonde and red hair blew in the wind. She was really beautiful, but she wasn't my type. I wanted my mate to be wild with a lot of spirit. She would be my equal in battle as well as the bedroom. I would know when I found her, and I hadn't found that special one yet.

I looked down and spotted Zoom and Lamont in the woods waiting for me. I passed them by and landed in a clearing, changing back into my human form. I was not hiding what I was; I just usually had to ease people into my supernatural form because there were not a lot like me. I came through the trees and I saw Lamont's green eyes glowing and Zoom's white eyes glowing. They were prepared to attack, and that made me feel better about the battles to come. We needed warriors right now; all of our lives depended on it.

Lamont ran over to me and grabbed Christy from my arms.

"Thank you for getting her for us. I have failed my nieces too many times, and I refuse to do it anymore," Lamont stated.

I slapped hands with Zoom, and he was on his cell phone telling his mate that we had her sister. I could tell that she was emotional because I heard her crying through the phone. I was happy that everybody wanted to celebrate, but we needed to get the hell out of these woods before the Seraphim and Esha figured out I killed Dantez. I was powerful, but I couldn't defeat a whole army by myself. Plus, I didn't know what the fuck was in Esha, and I didn't want to hang around and find out either. Plus, my energy was low from battling the Seraphim army before tracking Christy. I needed to feed and recharge soon, and that meant hunting.

"Yo, we need to head to Nichelle's house before they realize I killed Dantez. I am not trying to battle his army tonight," I said.

Zoom nodded his head after hanging up the phone and replied, "Yeah, you are right. Nichelle got on the phone and said that we needed to get Christy back there as soon as possible. They have a plan to stop Luke."

We all flashed by to my mama's house, and everyone was waiting for us in the living room. I went over and kissed my mother on the cheek, which surprised her, but she needed to get used to me, because I wasn't going anywhere since I had found my family. Zontae and Mesa better get used to me being around too. I needed to get to know my sisters and spend some quality time with them and my nieces and nephews.

Ever, of course, was fawning all over her sister and trying to wake her up from her potion coma. An older lady opened her purse and poured out a purple liquid and was about to pour the potion into Christy's mouth, but Ever stopped her.

"What the hell do you think you are doing? There is no way in hell that I am trusting Esha's mother, the queen of evil, to give my sister something, and I have no clue what it is. Someone else can give her something to wake up; you stay away from her!" Ever shouted.

"Bitch! I suggest you watch your tone when you are speaking to your elders. Now you may not like who or what she is, but you will respect her. All she is doing is trying to help your sister. Esha gave her a potion that is made from dark magic, and Madam Mary is the only one that understands how Esha works. So if you want your sister to wake up, I suggest that you shut the hell up and listen to what she has to say," the mystery woman stated.

Zoom stepped in between them and turned to Ever and whispered something in her ear. While he was calming her down, I was following the curves of the woman who currently had her hands on her thick hips. She was fucking gorgeous, and I loved her attitude because I couldn't stand a weak woman. I needed someone to challenge me. Fuck that obey me shit. I needed that arguing so we could fuck the hell out of each other afterward to get it all out and start again. I needed to know more about her.

"That's Lawrynn that you are staring hard at. Brother, don't stare too hard at her ass, I'm telling you. She turns into some shit I ain't never seen or heard about before. It's some kind of snake shit that creeps my ass out. Mess around in the middle of fucking her and her skin starts shedding or some shit. Naw, that ain't right at all. But then again, she might have that snake tongue that flicks real fast and shit on your dick. I don't know though; it's gambling with your life, messing with her," Mesa explained.

I laughed because this fool was always inappropriate. I heard him though, so I just nodded my head but kept my eyes on shorty. She might be my mate, who knows.

Ever finally let Mary give Christy the potion, and Christy instantly woke up fussing and crying. Her nagging ass was getting on my nerves. Nichelle came over and told me that they were taking Christy and the babies to the Fae Realm to protect baby Zai from the Forbidden Book and Christy from Esha. I was shocked to learn that Esha was the Forbidden Book. That explained her crazy ass talking to herself.

"So, you have a plan to kill Luke, but what about Esha? I know where her safe house is now, and I have eyes on her if she moves," I stated.

Mesa and Zontae looked at each other, and Zontae gave him a head nod.

"Grandma Black Witch here has a way to kill Esha and the Forbidden Book at the same time. So we have a way to do it; we just didn't know where Esha was hiding. Now that you have solved that for us, I say we try and get both of them today. Luke first, and then Esha. The faster we kill them, the less danger they are to baby Zai and the rest of the world," Mesa explained.

"She will do the ceremony tonight that will release the Forbidden Book, although she is unaware that is what she carries. The Dark One is good at deception, and I am sure that she thinks it's something else. It's a full moon tonight, and it will be searching for Christy and baby Zai to move into because I am sure that it is sensing that Esha's time is almost up on this planet. I am sure he hasn't informed her of that yet. Probably coaxing her with promises of power and who knows what else to get her to continue with her plans. We need to strike as soon as possible," Mary stated.

Zontae looked in deep thought and responded, "Lene, text Luke and get him to meet Jazz at her old condo. It's in the middle of nowhere and should be perfect to take him down once and for all.

Zeus, I know you need to head to the Demon realm to help Alpha and Omega with Syren's conversion. I think you need to take Dana with you so she can assist, and I am sure she needs some time with her daughter's death."

Zoom sat up and asked, "What the hell are you talking about? I thought Syren was upstairs with the babies?"

Nichelle explained what happened, and Zoom punched a hole in the wall.

"Your sons had no right doing that to my sister! I am going to whoop both of their asses as soon as they get back to this realm. As a matter of fact, take me to the fucking Demon realm so I can bring my sister back here where she belongs!" Zoom demanded.

Nichelle and Ever walked over to him, trying to calm him down. Hell, I understood where he was coming from. I just met my little sisters and would go to war over them. To find out your sister is mated to not one but two incubus demons, and she is now a succubus was a lot to deal with.

"Look, young man, I know you are upset about the actions of my sons, but you have to see that it was the only way that they could save your sister. They didn't even think about what they were doing. Their main focus was saving your sister and making sure that she survived the attack from Luke and his minions. She would be dead right now if it wasn't for them. Now I promise you that she is being well taken care of, for now she needs time to adjust, and so do you. I don't think it's a good idea for you to see her right now," Zeus stated.

Zoom's shoulders dropped as Ever rubbed his back. He closed his eyes and nodded his head after a few minutes.

"When she comes around, I need to see my sister. She and I are very close, and I know that she will need someone in her corner when she finds out what and who she has become. I want you to let your sons know that I want her treated with the respect that she deserves. She is not a sex toy for them to play with. I have heard about incubus and their demon reputations. I don't want her heart broken. She deserves mates that are faithful to her," Zoom replied.

Zeus nodded and responded, "I will make sure that she is treated with the utmost respect. She is my daughter now, and I won't have her disrespected. Just give me a chance to show you that we will take care of her."

They shook hands, and Zontae continued the conversation.

"Now, we need to split into two groups to handle everything. Nichelle, Lawrynn, Lamont, Zoom, Santonio, and Ever are going to take Christy and the babies into the Fae realm. Kaidan is meeting us here in a minute to help transport you safely there. We will meet up with Lawrynn and Zoom outside of the realm, to go after Esha. Lawrynn will be wearing Christy's clothes so that the demon dogs will pick up her scent and we can lead Esha into the woods to kill her and the book once and for all," Zontae directed.

"Excuse me, but I am not staying in some Fae world where I don't know anyone. What if someone tries to mate with me? I am not marrying someone with pointy ears. I'm just saying," Christy stated.

"Believe me, the last thing that any of my people are concerned about is marrying you," Kaidan said, stepping into the room.

Christy's mouth hung open as she stared at Kaidan's tall frame coming through the door. He bowed to Zontae and dapped up the fellows in the room except for Devin and Dane. No one really trusted them, and they definitely weren't cool with anyone in this room.

"Kaidan, how are things in your realm? Has anything improved?" Zontae questioned.

Kaidan's face turned grim, and he nodded his head 'no' and replied, "No. My people are still getting sick from an unknown source. Some of my guards said that Angel was spotted in the fields, but no one knows for sure, and our healers are working overtime to keep everyone alive and somewhat well."

Zontae shook his head sadly and responded, "As soon as we take care of Esha and Luke, I promise we will help the other realms out with their problems. I just wish there was more that I could do right now."

"No worries, believe me, we all want you to take care of Luke and Esha. There is nothing more important than that right now because we know they have a lot to do with what is happening to the other realms. I will take your people now and get them settled in my quarters. They will be my guests for the time being, and I will guard them with my life," Kaidan stated.

"It will be your life if something happens to my mama, nieces, or nephews... It will be your life," I stated with a straight face.

He nodded with a slight smile on his face, but he understood my meaning.

My sisters had tears in their eyes as they kissed their babies goodbye. Mesa and Zontae took them out of the room after they hugged our mama. When everyone left, it was just Nichelle and I standing. She pulled me into her arms and held on tight for a few moments before pulling away.

"Son, I need you to watch out for your sisters because they have targets on their backs as well as you. When this is all over, I want to spend some time with you and get to know what you have been up to. Although everything is very serious right now, I just want you to know how happy I am that you are alive and standing in front of me. Nothing will ever come between us again, Monroe. I love you," Nichelle stated.

I smiled and hugged her tight again and replied, "I will guard them with my life, Mama. I promise, as soon as this mess is over with, you and my family will have all my time. Just be careful, Mama. I love you."

She kissed me and headed out with her group. I just prayed that when we all met back up to finish Esha, there wasn't anyone missing from either group.

PART III
"CHOICES AND CONSEQUENCES"

"We all make mistakes. It's the way we accept and handle mistakes that makes a great leader."

— ZONTAE'

SYREN

I felt like I was floating on a cloud or high off a B- Pack. I was trying to wake up, but my eyes felt like they were glued shut. I sat back thinking about my last memory, and then it came to me. The fight between myself, Luke, and Jazz came flashing through my mind. I remember giving my magic to baby Zai and fading into the white light of the Spirit realm. I remember walking toward my mother, but she shook her head 'no' and told me it was not my time. She said that my husbands needed me, which was strange, because she added an 's' to the end.

I was brought out of my thoughts by voices that I recognized; I just couldn't figure out whose voices they were. I tried to open my eyes again, but they stayed shut. The voices got closer and became clearer. It was Alpha and Omega, and of course they were arguing.

"This is fucked up, and you know it. I think that you should leave and let me take care of her. I was the one that stepped to her first, and I should be the one to be her mate," Alpha stated, sounding like a petulant child.

I heard Omega sigh before he replied, "Alpha, she is my mate too. We didn't mean to change her into a succubus, but we did. We damn sure didn't know that we were both mating with her, but it happened.

Syren is not a toy that we need to fight over. When she wakes up, it's going to be hard for her to accept the changes to her body, let alone finding out that she is mated to two men that she barely knows. There is who does she like best or who should she choose. She will be hungry when she wakes up, and it is our responsibility to make sure that she is happy and healthy as our mate. Syren should be our main focus."

Alpha sucked his teeth and responded, "You are right. We will take care of her first, but after her feeding period, we will need to figure this shit out. Syren is mine, and I am not sharing with anyone, especially my brother. She's my other half, man; I feel it, and you know that I have never felt that way about any woman. Please, bruh, just let her go."

"We have a problem then, because I feel the same way about her also. You know that I love you and have always had your back and done everything that I could to make sure you were good. But I can't and won't give into you on this one, Alpha. Syren is my other half also. So, once she is good, we need to let her make the choice between us. We will stick by and honor her decision, no questions or arguments about it. Deal?"

There was a pause, and I was holding my breath, wondering what he would say. This whole situation was strange to me, and I was trying to wrap my mind around what they were saying about the situation I found myself in now. They must have found me and given me their blood to save my life. Now I am mated to two brothers and tearing them apart, not to mention, I am now a succubus.

"Deal. But whoever she doesn't choose has to move away from the Demon realm. Just in case there are residual feelings for that man. It's not fair to Syren, and her hormones might lead her to stray to that man," Alpha stated.

"Alright, deal. But that person can come to the Demon realm on holidays or special occasions as long as they promise not to touch Syren. It's not fair to the clan to be without its prince or king, especially now since we are at war and have no clue with whom," Omega stated.

"Shit, I'm hungry, bruh. We need to feed before she wakes up. She will already be in a frenzy; she doesn't need for us to be also. Yana and Natalie are available for a feeding session. I am texting them now to meet us in the blue room," Alpha said.

"Yeah, that will work, because I haven't fed in days, and I need to get this shit out before I kill somebody. After that, I might replace Natalie because she is starting to get too clingy. Yana might need to follow her since they are best friends," Omega stated.

Alpha laughed and replied, "Yeah, I feel you, but hell, that mouth got me stuck! But let's head in here and feed. Pops is on his way to help us figure out things here and to help out with Syren's transition."

I heard them get up and leave, but I was boiling. One minute these motherfuckers were fighting over me and professing their love, then the next minute they were talking about going to fuck some hoes! They had me fucked up! I was their mate, and they were supposed to stay faithful to me. I was lying in a coma, and they were up here talking about lying in some open pussy! Hell naw!

I concentrated and was willing my eyes to open. There was a rage growing inside of me that I never felt before. I was usually a mild mannered, calm person. But there was something inside of me that held such rage, and the thought of my mates fucking someone else had me hotter than fish grease. My left eye instantly popped open. It hurt at first because the light was bright in the room. A minute later, my right eye popped open, and I was trying to focus because everything was blurry. I sat up, and the world was spinning for a moment, but the energy inside of me allowed me to stand up.

The room was decorated in shades of purple, and I had to say it was beautiful. I walked over to the mirror, and I was shocked by what I was seeing. My eyes were dark red, and my body had changed drastically. My hips were wider, and my breasts were bigger and sat up more. My thoughts were interrupted by the giggles and moans that I heard coming from down the hall. I was naked, so I threw on the black silk robe that was left on the foot of the bed.

I walked down the hall and followed the voices, getting more and more pissed with each step. I felt something scrape my hand and realized that they were claws coming from my fingertips. I felt fangs scrape my bottom lip, and the anger became more intense.

I was breathing hard and growling as I came to the door that the voices and giggles were coming from. The rage took over, and I raised my leg and kicked the door in. Alpha had a petite girl sitting in his lap with her hand down his briefs, and Omega was standing up with a girl with natural curly hair all over her head twerking on his dick. They all were now staring at me.

Alpha and Omega, almost at the same time, pushed the hoes off them and came toward me. I growled at them, and they stopped.

The hoe that had been on Omega walked over with an attitude, but Omega pulled her back, which pissed me off more.

"Syren, look, it's not what you think. All they are is our food supply, nothing more. I need you to calm down, because you are in battle mode right now. You are what matters to us. We were just feeding now so when you woke up we could take care of you. Please let us explain before you go off," Omega stated in a calm voice.

Alpha was trying to ease up on my other side. Something else was growing inside of me the closer they came toward me. Lust and hunger started burning through my stomach and radiating down through my thighs, directly to my center, causing my clit to throb and my juices to start flowing and leaking onto my thighs.

I saw Omega stop, and he sniffed the air and closed his eyes. Alpha stopped also, and his eyes turned a dark red as he stared at me.

"Get the fuck out, Natalie and Yana!" Alpha growled.

Omega advanced on me and rubbed his nose on the side of my face, inhaling the scent of me with a moan. Alpha came to the other side of me and started running his fingers through my hair and kissing my neck.

I moaned, "Mmmmm, yes!"

"Are you kidding me! I can't believe you stopped trying to fuck us to get with this hoe!" Natalie yelled.

I reached around Omega and dug my claws into her skull and started dragging her out of the room.

"Let me go! Omega, help me!" Natalie yelled while she was kicking and screaming as blood ran down her face.

I looked over at Omega and Alpha with a look that dared them to interfere. Yana, or whatever her name was, stayed quiet and left with an attitude. I slung Natalie against the wall and slammed the door behind me.

My breathing was hitched, and I felt so much pressure in my body that needed to be released. I was sweating, and the fluids were leaking from my center as I stared at Alpha and Omega. They both had their shirts off and their bodies were on point with six packs and muscles everywhere. I wanted to lick every inch of their bodies.

"Syren, you are in heat. I know you are probably confused on what is going on right now, but you need to let us cool your body temp down before you overheat. Do you understand me?" Omega questioned, walking toward me.

I tried to focus on his voice, but all I could focus on was his dick print through his briefs. The last time I was intimate with someone was six months ago with Vice. Plus, this pressure and heat was really getting to me. I licked my lips in anticipation of the present that he had for me in his briefs. I untied my robe and let it drop. Both men groaned and growled as their eyes moved all over my naked body.

"Damn, you are going to make this harder for us than we thought. Look, we are going to take care of you, but we won't take it any further until after you can think for yourself. Right now, the heat has you," Alpha explained.

Did he just say I wasn't getting any dick? Aw, hell naw! I flashed over and ripped the briefs off both of them. I grabbed both of their dicks in my hands, and they had two of the longest and thickest butterscotch colored dicks I had ever seen. I started slowly moving my hands up and down their shafts and loved hearing them moan from the actions.

"Shit, Syren. This isn't how it was supposed to go," Omega growled out through his teeth.

I took his dick and placed it in my mouth and let the spit run down and get sloppy wet as I suctioned him into my mouth. I would come back up and suck on the head and make his knees weak. I felt a finger slide down and part my folds. It started slowly circling my clit. We moved toward the platform bed that housed tons of pillows. I placed Omega back in my mouth and went to work.

I realized that Alpha had slid up under me, and his face was directly under my thighs. He spread them apart, giving him easy access as his tongue slowly circled my clit and lapped up the juices that had been leaking earlier.

"Umm, I knew you would taste sweet. I have been waiting to taste you for a minute, Sy," Alpha said as his voice vibrated my clit, making me moan.

"Ssssssssss, suck on it, Alpha," I moaned and went down as much as I could on Omega's shaft, causing him to grab the back of my head and push me further down.

I felt something wet and slippery enter my walls. I realized it was Alpha's tongue extending inside of me and searching for that spot that would take me over the edge. Once his tongue found it, he started flicking it, alternating between fast and slow on my g-spot. Omega pulled himself out of my mouth and started sucking on my breasts as if he knew that the feeling of both points of pleasure would take me over the edge.

"Fuck! I'm cumming!" I screamed as I drenched Alpha's face with what felt like everything I had in me. Omega started kissing and licking my neck, which only increased the waves of pleasure that I was feeling. Once the waves subsided, my instincts kicked in, and I knew that my mates needed to be pleased.

I got up and spit on Alpha's dick and slowly went down on his shaft. I felt Omega rubbing his dick against my opening. My body reacted, and I helped him by making sure my curve was perfect and my ass was up. He inched into me, and I moaned as he made love to me slowly from behind.

"Shit, you are creaming all over my dick!" Omega moaned.

I started throwing it back as I sucked on Alpha's balls and licked up his shaft. His eyes were rolling up in his head, and I smiled knowing that I was the one to give him pleasure and not that hoe.

Alpha grabbed me by the hair when I put the head of his dick in my mouth, and started fucking my face.

"You about to catch all of our kids, and you bet not drop any of them either," Alpha said as he slid his dick in my mouth with his tip hitting the back of my throat, almost making me gag. The pre-cum leaked on to my tongue, and he was stiffening up and lengthening. I could tell that he was close to cumming, and I was going to savor every drop.

It felt so good to have them both in my body at once, and my orgasm was building with each slide of Alpha's dick on my tongue and every thrust of Omega inside my walls as he hit spots that had me going crazy. I started throwing it back like my life depended on it, as his pace increased along with Alpha's.

"Sy, I'm about to nut. You ready to catch this?" Alpha asked, and I nodded my head.

"I'm about to cum all in this good ass pussy," Omega moaned.

The way they were talking to me made me even more horny, and I felt the orgasm getting ready to peak. As my mates' movements became a frenzy, so did mine. We all peaked at the same time. I moaned against Alpha's dick in my mouth, and he shot his seeds down my throat. I felt Omega thrust hard into me one more time as his seeds shot deep within me. We all collapsed with Omega holding me from behind and Alpha holding me from the front. I was sandwiched between them and tried to catch my breath. I couldn't believe that I just had a threesome with Alpha and Omega. I should feel ashamed, but not as much as I thought I would.

I didn't know how all this was going to turn out, but for right now, I was going to throw away my worries and just enjoy the moment. That was my very last thought as Alpha slid inside of me with my leg in the crook of his arm. He stared into my eyes as Omega kissed my neck while rolling my nipples between his fingers. This was going to be a long pleasing night.

MARY

$\mathcal{W}$e were getting ready to leave and meet up to kill Luke. A lot of people wished to be able to see the future and know what was going to happen. I was not one of those people. Having the gift of sight was both a blessing and a curse. The Most High had forbidden me from telling my grandchildren what the future held. I was tired of the secrets and games that were being played in this battle between good and evil. I just hated that I was the one that started this mess, and I wished I could go back and change it, but I couldn't. All I could do now was to try and make up for all the wrong that I had done.

Lawrynn walked over to me, and I knew that she wasn't happy about leaving the cabin in the woods, but it was time for her to spread her wings. Plus, she had her own destiny to fulfill.

"I don't understand why I have to go and help guard these people when I should be guarding you. I don't think I should leave you with these people that have no respect for you. Especially the one with the dreads. I don't know why you don't zap him for calling you names," Lawrynn stated.

I laughed because Mesa was very disrespectful. He reminded me of Mathias, his grandfather. The good part of him at least.

"Don't pay any attention to him. He is just venting his feelings. How are you, my beauty?" I asked.

Lawrynn sighed and stated, "I am upset that you are sacrificing your life to save theirs. I know that you are their family, but so am I. I don't want you to leave me here alone."

I hugged her and replied, "You won't be alone. You will gain a new master and a new quest that will bring you happiness. All will be revealed soon, baby. Just have faith. Now, go and protect my great grandbabies, and I will meet up with you in the woods.

She smiled and gave me a kiss on the cheek and headed off down the path with the first group.

Samara walked over to me with a bottle of water, and I smiled. She was going to make a wonderful queen and wife to my grandson and the kingdom.

"Here you are, Ms. Mary. Are you sure that you don't want anything to eat before we head out?" she asked.

I smiled and replied, "No, baby, I am good. I ate before we came here. How is baby Zai?"

She looked sad and replied, "I'm not sure, to be honest with you. It scares me that he has some of the Forbidden Book in him and that he is able to use magic at his age. No offense, but I don't want him to turn out like Esha or you. I want him to be good, not evil."

I rubbed her back and responded, "The Forbidden Book doesn't make you evil, Samara. You have to have that in you before it can corrupt your soul. I was pregnant and corrupted my child in the womb, along with inviting the Dark One into her soul. Zai has two parents that are two of the most caring and loving people that I know. You just have to keep teaching him right from wrong and watching him closely. I sincerely believe that everything will work out. Now, I need to speak to your brother for a moment."

Samara looked at me strangely, then finally nodded her head and went off to get him. Monroe walked over to me and sat down beside me.

"Hello, Roe. I am glad that you have discovered your family. I know that you haven't revealed your true form yet. You should do so soon before the battle begins. You don't want to frighten them in the midst of battle and cause them to have hesitation that could get them killed," I stated.

He laughed and responded, "I should have known that the Black Witch would know what I am. But yes, you are right. I need to let them see before we are fighting Luke or Esha. Is there anything else you need?"

I handed him a necklace with a green glowing stone on the end. He took it and looked curiously at it.

"What is this?" he asked.

"I know you are a bounty hunter, and I need you to find someone for me after I am dead. Lawrynn doesn't know this, but she has a sister that I just found out about, apparently, hiding in the Forbidden realm. Her name is Latoya. When I pass on to the Spirit realm, I need you to go to my cabin. There is a letter there for Lawrynn and money to pay you for the job of finding her. One million dollars. The green stone will lead you to her once you are in the Forbidden realm. There is a catch, however, if you choose to take the mission," I explained.

Monroe smiled and replied, "There is always a catch, but I am going to take the job anyways. One million dollars is four times my fee. I would be crazy to turn down that amount of money, so go ahead and lay the catch on me."

"Lawrynn is a Kanima and has to have a master. When I pass on, she will become your responsibility. She is a warrior queen and will help you in capturing many bounties as your partner. She needs to feel like your equal, so don't underestimate her. Being her master only means that you need to be there for her. She won't be your slave or obey your every order. I want to make sure that she is taken care of, Roe. I know you are a good man and take your responsibilities seriously. You are what she needs," I stated.

Monroe ran a hand down his face and finally responded, "I can do that. When you move on to the Spirit realm, I will take over as her master and find her sister in the spirit realm. Now, let me speak to my sisters and everyone else and show them my true self. If no one else says it, thank you for your sacrifice."

I smiled and nodded my head. Monroe walked over to his sisters and the rest of the group and started talking. I watched as everyone's faces changed from curious to shock as Monroe explained what he was. I smiled because what the girls didn't know was that they would be able to take that form also.

Monroe changed from the handsome muscular man that they knew, into a huge fiery bird that no one had seen in centuries. He breathed fire into the air and took off with his wings flaming into the sky, leaving trails of smoke.

The Phoenix King was in full flame and ready to take on the world.

OMEGA

*W*e had been at it for hours, and finally Syren's heat had cooled down, and she was dead to the world. I picked her up, and we went to the bathroom where Alpha washed away the signs of our lovemaking, while I held her. Afterward, we moved her back into the purple room that was now hers as the queen of the Demon realm. Alpha pulled the sheets back, and I laid her down and covered her up. I placed a kiss on her lips as he placed a kiss on her forehead, and we backed out of the room.

As soon as we were out, Alpha and I headed our separate ways to shower and meet up in our office downstairs. I knew we needed to talk about what just happened. We had originally agreed that when Syren woke up, we wouldn't do anything but ease her heat with our tongues. We were not supposed to take it there and fully make love to her, but that is exactly what we did. Being inside of her was like nothing I had ever felt before. If I didn't know it before, I knew it now. Syren was meant to be my mate.

I finished showering and threw on a pair of basketball shorts and a white tank top. I headed downstairs and into our office. I popped a B-Pack to calm my nerves, lit a blunt, and poured myself a shot of

Blennessy. I knew this conversation was going to go left quickly with my brother, but there was no way I was letting Syren go.

When Alpha walked in, he had on basketball shorts and a tank also; this was just how we were. We thought alike and watched out for each other. When Pops wanted to pick who would be king, we ended up sharing the position. We had never had a situation where we argued or disagreed on anything until Syren came into our lives. Now I wasn't sure if I was going to lose my brother or not.

Alpha poured himself a drink and sat down at the other desk that was in the room. He looked up at me and shook his head.

"We have a problem, don't we, bruh," Alpha stated.

I chuckled and nodded my head. "Yeah, we do. I think we both know that making love to Syren changed everything that we had planned. I feel in my heart that she was meant to be my mate. I don't want to fight you, Alpha, but I will do what I need to do in order to keep her."

"Well, the problem is, when I was inside of her, I felt the same thing. She is everything I have ever wanted in a woman and more. I can't walk away from her, even if she wants you more. Hell, I won't walk away from her either, so I guess we are at an impasse," said Alpha.

"I still feel her legs wrapped around me. I swear her shit is like a drug, and I wanted more, but she was tired. We will need to speak with her after she wakes up and has a clearer mind about what she wants to do. I'm sure she will have questions, and we need to keep our dicks in our pants so she can answer them," I stated.

Alpha started laughing and said, "Natalie and Yana I know are pissed the fuck off by being tossed too. You know Natalie wasn't expecting that shit. I guess we should have explained that we have a mate now. Their job as food has dried up quickly after I had a taste of Syren. Hell, I don't want anyone else but her, and I haven't ever had that feeling about anyone."

"I feel a little bad about Natalie because I did promise her a chance to be my mate if I didn't find one by my birthday. I need to have a chat with her and explain some things so she understands what happened. I owe her that much," I said.

"Omega, you are too fucking nice. You need to leave that ditzy ass broad where she is before she causes more trouble between you and Syren. Hell naw, fuck that! Yeah, go ahead and see her so Syren will be pissed off and I can get some solo pussy. Do you, bruh," Alpha said with a smile.

He was probably right, but I felt obligated to let her know in person. She had been more than food to me; she had been a friend. We were about to grab another drink, when our father walked in looking grim, and Dana was tagging along behind him.

"What's up, Pops? Why are y'all looking so sad?" Alpha asked.

"I have some news that you all need to hear. Dana, there are five guest bedrooms upstairs. You can take any of them and make yourself at home," Zeus stated while rubbing her face.

My brother and I exchanged glances as he caressed her face and kissed her on the forehead.

"Thanks, Zeus. I am just tired and hurt that I couldn't help Jazz. No matter what she had done, she was still my child," stated Dana.

THIS WAS the first I heard of it. I had no clue that Jazz was dead and how she died. To be honest with you, I was not surprised because of the company that she kept. It was just a matter of time before she found her way into a grave.

"You have my condolences, Mrs. Dana. Let us know if there is anything we can do, " I said as she started walking toward the staircase. She nodded with a small smile and continued upward.

Pop's eyes followed her all the way up, and then he turned his attention to us. He told us about the plans that Zontae had for Luke and Esha. They were solid but definitely had risks. I just wanted those motherfuckers dead at any cost to be honest with you.

"Have you found out what or who has been killing our people and dropping them all over the city?" Zeus asked.

"No. We have people out gathering information, but no one has witnessed anything. Also, there is no clear pattern with the killings. I want to say this has Esha all over it. All of the realms are being attacked. It's like she planned a coordinated attack on all the realms at once," Alpha stated.

Zeus nodded his head and replied, "That's exactly what she did, son. I am just not sure who she sent into our territory. How is Syren? I brought Dana to help in case she needs a female to talk to."

Alpha and I looked at each other and smiled.

"She woke up early this morning in heat. We took care of her, and now she is resting," I stated.

Zeus looked between both of us and shook his head.

"So, the both of you took care of her. So how is this going to work out in the long run? She was horny when she woke up, but when she wakes up this time, her mind will be clear. You both need to be prepared that her mindset might be totally different when she comes to terms with her new circumstances. All I am saying is be prepared to have your hearts broken, and take it like a man," he explained.

There was a knock on the door, and I said come in. It was Blane, our right hand, and he had a CD in his hand.

"Kings, this was left on the doorstep. I haven't watched it, but I figured you needed to see it."

I popped the CD into the computer, and the guy named Vice from Cas's gang popped up.

"I know you were wondering who was dropping bodies in your territory. Well, look no further. Queen Esha sends her regards and wants you to know that you should have picked the winning side. But, I have a personal stake in the matter. See, you have something precious to me, and I want it back! I am talking about Syren. She belongs to me, and you and your stupid ass brother stole her from me. You have two days to return her to me, or I will kill someone closer to you. Return my mate or else," he stated, and the video ended.

"Did he just say return his mate?" Alpha questioned.

I nodded my head 'yes' and sat back in my chair. How could Syren be his mate when she was ours?

JADE

*H*ave you ever had one of those moments where you regretted the choices that you made? Or when the consequences of your actions were so severe and scary that you wanted to run and hide? That was the situation that I found myself in right now. You see, I have always wanted to be in power. I wanted to be the queen that ruled over the Underworld. That was the main reason that I fought so hard to have Zontae. He was fine, don't get me wrong, and his lovemaking was off the charts, but power was what gave me orgasms. Now I wished that I had never taken Esha's side.

I had tried to phone my father, but he wasn't answering. I was balled up in the corner of a motel room where I had fled ever since the events that happened earlier. My body was bruised with black and blue marks covering my light skin. My body was sore from being used in ways that I never thought were possible.

You see, a few hours ago, my life took a turn for the worst in a way I had never thought would happen. Hell, no one would even believe me if I told them. The shit was too weird and it was a nightmare come true. I used my phone and looked to see how much money I had in the bank. I had two hundred thousand, so I could live off that, especially since I wanted to move to Mexico.

I tried phoning Jazz, but I couldn't find her either. I left a text telling her to get out of town and not to go anywhere near Esha or whatever the hell she was. I gathered the strength to get off the floor and pulled on the hat to hide my face and the bulky clothes to hide my body. It was time to leave Nashville and never come back. I thought about what Zontae told me the day of the burial ceremony, and he was right. We used to be friends, and I threw that all away for that crazy bitch!

I picked up the phone and dialed Zontae. I fully expected him not to pick up because of our history, but surprisingly, he answered.

"What do you want, Jade?" he asked with an attitude.

"Hey, Zontae. I don't have long to talk because I am trying to get as far away from Esha as I can. I just had to warn you that your mother is not the same anymore. Something is possessing her because Esha is not the same; she has been taken over by the devil. Don't go up against her because I am not sure that you will win. She knows that you are sending Christy to the Fae realm. She found a way to seal the entrance. Kaidan won't be able to get in, and she will get Christy. She wants Christy so she can have some type of super heir or some weird shit. I might not be a good person, but no one should be subjected to that shit. I am leaving town, Tae, you don't have to worry about me anymore. You were right; it wasn't worth it," I said with tears running down my face.

"You alright, Jade? Are you in danger?" he asked.

I would love for him to come to my rescue, but it was too late. The damage had been done and I was ready to move on and away from this madness. I needed normal.

"No, I am okay. Just listen to my advice and take care of your beautiful babies. I am sorry for the trouble that I caused. Please apologize to Samara for me. Watch out for Jazz for me, and try and get her to follow a better path also," I said.

I heard him take a deep breath, and he replied, "Jade, Jazz tried to kill my kids and niece. I'm sorry, but she isn't around anymore."

The tears started flowing at the loss of my sister. I couldn't believe that she tried to kill babies, but look who our father was. Now, I knew in my heart it was time to leave. There was nothing holding me here anymore.

"It's okay, Zontae. I wish you well, and watch out for Esha. Thanks for being my friend, even when I wasn't to you. Have a good life," I stated as I hung up the phone.

I flashed to the bank and cleared out my accounts and went to a second one and cleared out Jazz's. We looked so much alike that it was easy to do. I had half a million in my bag and hopped in the car that I had bought with cash. It was time to get lost before Esha came looking for me. I had something that she wanted and couldn't have. Goodbye Nashville.

SAMARA

We were in the trees waiting on Luke to get here. Selene was laying on the ground like she was passed out. She was wearing Jazz's clothes and a blonde wig. I felt the buzz of magic and power that Nichelle had passed along to me, Selene, and Monroe. Hell, my brother didn't look like he needed it. His ass was a huge fiery bird that scared the hell out of me. Mary told Selene and I that we had the same spirit inside of us; we just had to dig deep to bring it out.

The plan was for Zontae, Mesa, and Zaire, to subdue him and Devin, Dane, and Selene I would combine our magic and kill him. Luckily, he only had a small portion of the book in his body. Sad thing was he was under the impression that he had the majority of those powers. It was really sad how people were so blinded by power that they ended up missing out on the things that were right in front of them.

The person that I was worried about stopping was Esha. This bitch had the Forbidden Book in her and had no clue that she did. She had been living with it in her body all her life. There was a ceremony that we had to perform in order to stop the black book and her. I just hated that Ms. Mary had to sacrifice herself in order to stop Esha.

Zontae and Mesa weren't saying too much, but it had to be affecting them in some way that their grandmother had to burn to death when they were just getting to know her.

I looked across the field at Zontae as he answered his phone. He looked to be in deep conversation with someone and had a worried look on his face. It looked like he was about to say something, when all of a sudden, Luke appeared beside Selene.

Mesa and Zontae got prepared to grab him. But before they could, he had grabbed Selene up by her shoulders, realizing it wasn't Jazz.

"Where is my daughter?" Luke screamed as he shook Selene.

Selene smiled and replied, "In hell where you will be soon!"

Luke growled, and he focused his gaze on Selene, and I saw her getting paler. He was somehow draining her of her magic.

Devin tackled his father and Selene. Luke grabbed onto Devin and started sucking the magic out of him. Dane shot him with his blue gaze, but Luke just kept siphoning Devin. I levitated in the air and threw a boulder that I saw on the ground not too far away.

"Watch out, Lene!" I yelled and watched Mesa flash and grab her before it could hit her. It hit Luke and knocked him over. Dane ran to help his brother, but it was too late. He tried to pick up Devin's body, and it turned to dust because Luke had literally sucked the life out of his own son.

"Noooooo! You sick ass motherfucker! You killed your own son!" Dane yelled with tears falling down, on his knees, staring at the remains of his brother. I had never seen him show as much emotions as he was showing now. Devin gave his life to save my sister, and I was glad that he was there to help her. I remember we always wanted to get away from him, but I didn't want him to lose his life, no matter what he had done to us.

The boulder started moving, and I pointed to it and said, "He's trying to climb out!"

Mesa, Zontae, and Zaire started circling the boulder, getting into position. No matter which way he came out, one of them would be there to whoop his ass.

He came out on Zaire's side and stared at Zaire in shock.

"Zaire, how are you alive? I was there when Esha beheaded you!" Luke said in shock.

Zaire laughed and replied, "Next time you should make sure that you are killing the right person, you stupid motherfucker! You were supposed to be my best friend, and you gave all that up for Esha's mediocre open house pussy. We were supposed to make a difference in the Underworld, but instead, you have done everything in your power to destroy it. Then, you tried to kill your own godsons for power. Not to mention, you just killed your own son. You a scandalous asshole, and that's putting it mildly."

Zaire hooked off and punched Luke in the face. They started going back and forth, trading shots. But clearly, Zaire was getting more hits in. Every time Luke would try and use his magic, Zaire would punch him in the eyes. Zaire bit a chunk out of Luke's neck, and the blood started flowing. Luke kicked Zaire in the stomach and was about to deliver a blow to the head, when Zaire gained his composure and sliced a deep gash across Luke's chest and neck. Blood was pouring from Luke everywhere. Luke's eyes were almost swollen shut, and Zaire was standing there with his knuckles bleeding and his chest heaving. Luke tried to use his magic, but he was too weak, and only a small amount came out, sizzling on the ground. He hung his head in defeat and faced Zaire.

"I was in love with her! You weren't! All you wanted was Nichelle! And all I ever wanted was Esha. I was going to give her the world, and you were in the way! I loved you like a brother, but I loved Esha more. You didn't deserve her; she was meant for me. She is a queen, and I needed to be king so she could have her crown, and you were in the way!" Luke yelled.

Luke must have been recharging his powers because he started shaking, and his eyes started glowing. I knew he was building his magic up to use it on Zaire. I tapped Lene on the arm, and we put our hands together and concentrated on Luke. He had started building an energy ball and was about to hurl it at Zaire. Lene stopped the ball with her mind, and I added lightning bolts and fire to it. Lene sent it back into Luke, and it knocked him off, absorbing into his body. You could hear his body crackling from the inside with the electrical shocks from the bolts like a taser. The fire was burning him on the inside, and he was screaming.

"Ahhhhhhhh!" Luke thrashed around on the ground in agony.

"He's getting on my fucking nerves with all that damn screaming and shit like a bitch!" Mesa said as he punched a hole in his chest, ripping his heart out. Zontae ripped his head off and tossed it on the ground.

I noticed the black cloud leaving his body, which I knew was the piece of the Forbidden Book.

"Mara, trap that black shit if you can!" Zontae yelled.

I frowned but formed a clear bubble with a hole in it and placed it in front of the moving smoke. It flowed in, and I sealed the hole up. I placed more white magic around it to hold it in place. The black smoke kept bumping against the material, trying to get out.

"Let me help," Mary stated.

She walked over and said a few words over the bubble. It immediately stopped moving and stayed in the middle of the bubble. She made the bubble smaller and gave it to me to place in my pocket.

"That should hold it until we can get to Esha and complete the ceremony," Mary explained.

"Daughter, help your father-in-law out and set his scandalous ass on fire," Zaire said.

I raised my hand and set his body, heart, and head on fire until it was nothing but ashes left.

"We got to get over to the clearing. Jade called and said that Esha knows about our plans to move Christy and has found a way to seal the portal to the Fae realm. We have to go now before she gets her hands on Christy and the babies!" Zontae yelled and flashed away.

"Y'all go ahead. I need to prepare a burial ceremony for my brother," Dane said solemnly. I wanted to say something to him, but what do you say to someone that has lost his brother and best friend?

Selene and I grabbed Mary's hand and flashed to the clearing where we were supposed to meet up with Zoom. When we got there, Zontae, Zaire, and Mesa were standing still on the clearing's edge. The sight that met us had me holding my breath and praying that we didn't end up like Devin—dead and turned to dust.

ZONTAE

*E*sha was standing there with a dagger pressed into Nichelle's throat, and there was a large Seraphim army behind her. Christy had baby Zai in her arms, and Ever had Mena and Zaniyah. Zoom, Lamont, and Lawrynn were standing in front of Ever and Christy, guarding them, waiting for anyone or anything to attack.

Slice was standing off to the side looking for an opportunity to grab Nichelle, and Kaidan was in between, ready to dive and help out in either situation. Esha smiled as she saw me taking in the whole scene.

"Well, if it isn't my children all together in one place. How heartwarming. I was really hoping that one or two of you would be dead by now, but no. You just had to keep hanging around like cockroaches. I thought my sons would be my heirs, but instead, they ended up being trash like their weak ass daddy," Esha said with a smile.

"Naw, you are not offending me Hoe-Esha. I mean, it's not that I was a pushover, I just didn't give a fuck about you. I was more upset that my friends had betrayed me than you lying there with your legs cocked open for the whole council to stick their dicks in and sling their nut in. I mean, that is all that you are good for, catching nuts in every fucking hole that's open in your body. It's a wonder you can hear or see without cum oozing out of your eyes or ears."

Esha looked mad for a moment and then her face changed. It was subtle, but I noticed. A deep voice came from her body, and I knew it had to be the Forbidden Book or the Dark One. I didn't care which one; I was just ready to get this shit over with.

"I just need to impregnate Christy here and then you can have her back. I mean, I only had them to carry my heirs. The cells that I injected them with had vampire, shifter, angel, and demon cells in them. My son that I put in her, should reign supreme over the Underworld. My daughters may look and act human, but they are anything but. Their nature just has been suppressed. Now that Ever has been mated, it should be interesting to see what she becomes. But really, I just created them to be incubators or surrogates as you say, for my true son. Otherwise, they are completely useless. Just give me a day with her, and you won't have to die right now along with your babies."

"If you touch our babies, I promise you that you won't even get five steps without dying yourself. I will make sure that you boil alive in your own skin, whatever and whoever the fuck you are," Samara stated, getting closer to the babies.

"Just like your mother; all mouth and no action. I wish that I had killed you and your line a long time ago. You have done nothing but caused trouble for my family. That's why I am going to slice your mother's throat and drink her blood until I drain her, then I will have a go at you and your sister. Maybe I can place a baby in you, Samara; the child would be amazing. Plus, I could fuck the shit out of you while my son watches," Esha stated.

"What the fuck? You do know that you don't have a dick, right, Esha? You are talking real crazy right now. Not to mention, your voice deeper than mine! What the fuck are you on?" Mesa asked.

Selene was sneaking toward the back of the Seraphim army that was trying to get to the babies and Christy. I saw her and Mara giving each other a look, then she glanced over at Monroe, who was doing the same thing. Those three were up to something; I just didn't know what. We had to keep Esha's attention off them.

"Son, my dick is probably bigger than yours. You have no idea of what I am capable of," Esha replied.

Mesa looked disgusted and replied, "Now that's just nasty. Pops, you didn't notice a dick down there when you was fucking her? I'm all for rainbow rights, Pops, if that's what floats your boat, but this shit here is on some other level shit."

"Eshena, it's time for your games to end. We have both caused enough trouble in the world," Mary said, stepping around from behind Samara. I saw the stunned look on my mother's face. The tough act dropped for a moment, and it was the first time I saw actual fear cross her face, and then the mask was back in place.

"Mother, I thought your old ass had died. What are you doing here with the enemy? Do you have dementia or something? Need help with your Depends or some Icy Hot?" Esha said with a smile.

Mary shook her head and replied, "You are not my daughter. You are the Dark One who has possessed her and stole her soul. Why are you pretending to be something that you are not? We both know that you are so arrogant that you placed the Forbidden Book inside of her so you would be close to it because you don't trust anyone. You want an heir so you can walk this earth and cause havoc. Esha's body must be growing weak, and that's why you want out. She's not powerful enough for you. She can be destroyed."

Esha smiled and replied, "You think that I don't have backup plans for my backup plans? Even when you think you have stopped me, I am already five steps ahead. I am not foolish to think that I can cause all this chaos by myself. No. I have many that are more than willing to serve me and my cause. I mean, we must keep the destined Phoenix Queens and Kings busy with evil so they can fulfill their destiny, right? I have already started my plans in each of the realms with the help of my servants. The trouble they are out causing now will be felt for years and centuries to come. Where you think I have failed, Mother Dearest, I have already won. I created a new breed of Underworlders that are even, now as we speak, walking around the humans, waiting to pounce and do what they were trained to do. Every realm is feeling my wrath, so get ready. Now, I am getting sick of talking. It's time to end this so I can take my prize and go and make plans to dominate the world."

Esha waved her hand, and the Seraphim army started to attack. Esha sliced Nichelle's throat, and her body dropped. I heard my father screaming as he ran to her body.

"Nichelle!" Zaire screamed as he sliced through Seraphim with his blessed sword trying to get to her.

I pulled out both of my blades as well as Mesa, and we started slicing through them trying to get to the kids and Christy. I saw them, and Lawrynn and Zoom were fighting Seraphim, trying to keep them away. Lawrynn was in her Kanima form and was slicing them and filling them with venom, and they were dropping like flies.

Zoom stepped into the clearing, and his eyes turned snow white. He lifted his hands and placed a protective blue bubble around Ever and Christy. I watched as Seraphim bounced off and attempted to break through. He raised his hands and sent out a wave of white light that took out half the Seraphim army.

I smiled and continued to battle and take down the ones that were closest to me. One of the Seraphim was about to stab Zoom in the back.

"Zoom! Watch out behind you!" I yelled, but I knew it would be too late.

Lamont stepped in behind Zoom, and the blade went through his chest into his heart.

"Uncle Lamont, noooooooooooo!" I heard Ever scream.

He lifted his hand and smiled before dropping and disintegrating into ashes.

"Fuck!" I yelled out as we continued to battle the Seraphim until the last one fell dead.

I looked over at Mesa, and we were both breathing hard and were covered in blood and ashes.

I looked over, and Zaire had Nichelle in his lap, feeding her his blood.

Samara, Selene, Monroe, and Mary had formed a circle around

Esha and were chanting some words, keeping her in a circle of white light as she screamed.

"Let me out, you bitches! You can't hold me for long, and when I get out, I am going to eat your babies alive!" Esha yelled.

Mara stepped through the circle and grabbed Esha by the throat and punched her in the nose, knocking her on her knees. I heard a crack, and I knew her nose was broken. Blood was pouring from her nose, but she just kept laughing until Mara held her mouth open, and Lene stepped forward, raising her hands and mentally started pulling Esha's tongue out until it ripped off and fell to the ground. It started crawling away like an inchworm.

"Fuck you, bitch! Talk that shit now without a tongue!" Lene yelled.

Esha stood and used magic to blast Mara and Lene back out of the circle, with them landing with a thud onto the ground. She stood and smiled and raised her hand. The skies turned black and the wind picked up. She picked up her tongue and placed it back in her mouth.

"Is that all that you stupid bitches got!" Esha yelled.

Mesa and I looked at each other and ran into the circle, stabbing Esha with the blessed swords in the back and the side. The wounds started sizzling immediately and Esha hissed. We drew her attention to us as Mary sprinkled the herbs around the circle.

"Get out now! Samara, toss me the bubble!" Mary shouted at us. Mara tossed the bubble, and Mary caught it. She sprinkled the last of the herbs, and the circle closed as soon as we rolled out.

Esha ran around, trying to get out, but the barrier would not let her out.

"Why are you doing this to me, Mother? You hate them as much as I do! We could rule together and squash them all!" Esha screamed.

Mary walked over to Esha and laid a hand on her cheek.

"I ruined you and let him take my precious baby girl's soul. You could have been so much more, but I allowed my hate to eat away at my soul and yours. It's time that we answer for everything that we have done and atone for our sins. No matter what you have become, I love you, Eshena."

Monroe, Lene, and Mara joined hands and started chanting. The ground shook, and the earth started to crack. Mesa and I ran over to the babies to make sure that the shield was holding, and it was.

I watched as Monroe changed into a huge Phoenix, still holding on with his eyes closed, then Lene and Mara changed into Phoenixes, something that they had never done before. They weren't as large as Monroe, but they were just as powerful. The flames from their body caught the circle on fire, and I watched as it formed a bubble of heat, and Esha and Mary started to sweat heavily. Our grandmother was staring at us with a smile. I felt a tear roll down my face as it hit me that she was about to die, and I didn't get to really know her.

"Don't shed tears for me, grandsons. I am relieved and at peace now. I can't do anything else to hurt you or anyone else. Just watch out for your sisters and your children. The Dark One will only be temporarily stopped for now. He will come back with vengeance one day. I love each and every one of you. Lawrynn, honey, stop crying. I have chosen a new master for you, and he will take care of you and guide you. Listen to him because he speaks the truth," Mary stated.

"Fuck all of you! You will pay for doing this to me! You think you have stopped me, but you have only angered me more! Just wait until my retribution comes for you and your bloodline! You think this is the end, but it's only the beginning!" Esha yelled out and started laughing as her face turned monstrous, something between a dragon and a dog.

"Forgive me, my child," Mary stated as she plunged the fiery dagger through Esha's heart. Esha screamed as she started melting until there was nothing but bones left.

Mary stabbed herself in the heart and turned to ashes. The fire continued to burn until there wasn't anything left. The fire hit the black smoke that was the Forbidden Book, and it screamed as it was set on fire and reduced to ashes.

Once the fires burned out, Monroe, Lene, and Mara returned to their normal selves. They each fell to the ground, unconscious and bloody from having used so much power.

"Lawrynn, can you take Christy, Ever, and the babies back to the house?" Mesa asked.

Lawrynn nodded her head 'yes' and replied, "Yes, of course. I will guard them with my life. Mary would want me to protect her family."

Mesa and I nodded as she guided them to the path to flash them home.

"Kaidan, can you carry Monroe back to the castle so he can rest? Also, Slice, take Lamont's body back to the house so we can give him a proper burial. Pops, how is Nichelle?" I asked.

"She barely has a pulse. I gave her as much blood as I could and sealed the wounds. There had to be some type of poison on the dagger because it is making her sick and slowing the healing," Zaire stated.

He gently picked her up and placed a kiss on her lips. He flashed away toward the house.

I grabbed Mara, and Mesa grabbed Lene. They were still knocked out, but that was to be expected. They had saved us and our children. We had lost some of our people in this battle; some were injured and weak, but the main thing was that we won. We were here to fight another day.

"Now, King Zontae, it's time to figure out how to stop the chaos in the other realms. Not to mention, we have the coronation to get through. Are you ready for this?" Mesa questioned.

I smiled, even though the situation ahead of us was filled with problems.

"As long as you are beside me, along with our mates, I am as ready as I will ever be," I stated. We flashed to the house to rest and prepare for the next chapter.

"THE AFTERMATH"

"Have you ever thought that things were going too perfect? You start wondering when the bad shit was going to come and fuck everything up? Well, that is how I have been feeling for a minute. Unsettled."

— SELENE.

SELENE

*T*adjusted the crown on my head, reminding me that I had now been crowned Princess of the Underworld. The ceremony was beautiful and a long time coming. It had been three months since that day in the clearing where we destroyed Esha. I was not going to lie and say that I didn't have nightmares from that day because I did. I was currently bouncing Mesa Jr. on my lap, trying to get him to go to sleep. He was demanding like his father and wanted all of my attention. Mena was sweet and patient, which helped me out.

Cora Lee, our nanny, came and got him as soon as he was asleep. She was a Fae that was a grandmother fifty times over, and the kids seemed to love her, even baby Zai who was cautious of everyone.

My mother still hadn't recuperated from the poison that Esha dosed her with. She would only wake up for an hour or two. She was so weak that the only thing she could keep down was Zaire's blood, which was causing my father Santonio to become angry and resentful. We were searching all over for a cure for her, but so far, nothing had worked.

Dana and Zeus are away traveling. After losing both her daughter and her son, she had a mental breakdown. Zeus thought it would be good to get her away from Nashville for a while, so he took her on a world tour. He was not pushing to be in a relationship until he thought that she was healed.

"What are you thinking about, baby? Me hitting it from the back so we can work on baby number three?" Mesa questioned, coming up behind me.

I smiled and leaned into him and replied, "You, sir, are going to have to wait for baby number three. Your babies have big heads like you, and it hurts pushing their big head asses out."

He mushed me in the head, and I started laughing.

"My babies don't have big heads. They just are smart as hell and have big brains. Don't hate because your family have almond shape heads. Nutty ass family," Mesa stated while laughing. I pushed his ass for talking about my family. He grabbed my hands and kissed each one.

"But seriously, you were in deep thought. What were you really thinking about?" Mesa questioned.

"My mother and Dana. I just hate that Esha and Luke's shit messed them up. They are still suffering, and there is nothing I can do. I miss my mother, and it's hard seeing her that way. I just wish we could find the cure," I explained.

Mesa hugged me tight and responded, "We will find it, baby. I promise you that we will get your moms right. Now, I have to get to the meeting of the realms. Why don't you lay down and take a nap? I have a feeling that baby number three is already in there with your emotional ass. Now go on and wait on daddy to come back and make that pussy talk with her spitting ass."

I laughed because my husband was one of a kind. Meeting Mesa had changed my life, and I wouldn't have it any other way.

SAMARA

I was sitting here going through my mother's and Mary's spell books, trying to find anything to help my mother to get better. I had taken the heavy crown off that had made me Queen of the Underworld a while ago. I rubbed my back and felt a pair of hands start taking over and rubbing the kinks out of my back, as he moved them on to my swollen belly.

"What are you doing in here? Don't you have a meeting with the realm right now?" I asked.

Zontae was still dressed from the coronation in an all-black custom suit that fit his body to a tee. The heavy crown was sitting atop his head, gleaming in the light, with the diamonds and emeralds that decorated the crown.

"I had to make sure that you weren't overdoing it with all the events that went on today. I had Cora Lee draw you a bath, and there is a peanut butter and jelly sandwich waiting on you upstairs. I know how much my new son loves them," he stated, rubbing my belly.

I rolled my eyes and replied, "You do know that this could be a little girl, right?

He chuckled and said, "Naw, Zaniyah is the only princess around here. This little one in your belly is Zontae Jr. Now head upstairs and get some sleep before I come up there and forget all about a meeting."

"I will in five minutes. I need to just go through this last book. Plus, Ever is headed up here, and I wanted to see if she found anything," I explained.

Zontae looked sad for a moment and responded, "Alright. But seriously, Mara, just a few more minutes. You know Nichelle would be pissed if you put her grandbaby in danger. I love you, and I will be up here later to rub your crusty feet."

I laughed and threw one of the books at his head, which I knew he would catch, and of course he did. He blew me a kiss and left.

Ever came in, and she had spit up on her, which I was sure came from Aria, her and Zoom's daughter.

"Sorry I was late. Zai and Aria did not want to go down. I don't see how Cora Lee watches all of them. I am exhausted. Did you find anything?" Ever asked.

I shook my head 'no' and replied, "Not one thing that would help us out in finding a cure or the cause. I feel like I am running out of places to look, and I have no clue how to cure my mother. I feel like she is wasting away."

Ever grabbed my hand as I wiped the tears from my eyes.

"I am not giving up. There has to be something. Monroe said that he overheard my mother talking about my blood and Christy's blood being able to heal people. We can start there and give her some of my blood or Christy's blood. If that doesn't work, we can keep looking," Ever stated.

Ever had been looking into her blood for a while now to see what Esha had done to her and her sister. She was waiting for results to come back from a shifter that specialized in DNA.

"Maybe I can help," Dane said, stepping into the room.

Dane had been in mourning for the past three months since his sister, father, and brother had died. Of course, it was more so his brother that caused him the most pain because they were very close.

"Dane, you know that Zontae will be upset if he catches you in here. Please leave," I stated. I didn't want his death on my hands.

"I am not here for that or to cause trouble. I really want to help to make up for all the things that I have done to you and your sister. Look, Esha dealt in black magic and more than likely, that's where the spell or curse came from. I can go into the Dark Forest and find out what the poison or curse could be and bring back a cure. My brother is gone, and I have been exiled from the coven. I need a purpose and something to keep my mind off his death so I can heal. Please, as your subject, let me go off on a mission for my queen," Dane stated with tears in his eyes.

I thought about it, and I knew that Zontae was going to whip my ass for this, but I got the feeling that Dane really wanted to atone for his sins and help my mother.

"Fine. You can go on a mission to save my mother. Please don't make me regret this, Dane, or I promise, you will be joining your brother in the Spirit realm, do you understand me?" I asked.

He nodded his head 'yes,' and for the first time in a long time, I saw a sparkle in his eyes.

"Yes, my queen, I understand, and I won't let you down. Thank you!" He bowed and left the room.

"You know that you have a big heart, right? But your man is going to whoop your ass when he finds out," Ever stated.

I smiled at her, but I knew she was right. Zontae would be mad at first, but he would understand it was for my mother. Sometimes we had to make tough decisions that our loved ones won't like.

MONROE

I had been training Lawrynn for the past three months on how to handle herself against certain creatures that she hadn't come up against before. She was a quick learner but was also stubborn as hell. I had held off on giving her the letter until I knew that she was fully trained and ready to accompany me through the Forbidden Realm to find her sister.

That realm was not for the faint at heart, and I needed her to be on her shit if we were to make it out of there alive.

I went to grab her shoulder, and she stepped on my foot and hip tossed me to the ground. At the last minute, I grabbed her and made her land on top of me. Big mistake on my part because I felt all of her curves and breasts against my body. My third leg started to thump against her center that was pressed directly on it.

Lawrynn smiled and said, "If you wanted to do another type of exercise, you should have told me. I mean, as long as there are no strings attached that is. I wouldn't want you getting strung out on the good stuff that I have between my thighs. I don't do cuddling either."

I pushed her off my body and stood up. She always said things that threw me off my game, and it was starting to get on my nerves.

"I don't mess around with little girls. I am more interested in women. Now if you are finished training and imagining shit for the day, I need to give you something that I have been holding on to until I felt like you were ready for it," I explained.

She grabbed my dick and started massaging it, which almost made me moan it felt so good.

"Well, I am ready for it. I just don't think you are ready for me, little boy," Lawrynn whispered in my ear.

I stepped back and adjusted myself because this conversation was going to end up with us going places that I didn't want to go with her.

"Naw, it's not that. I have a letter from Mary that she wanted me to give to you. I held on to it until I thought you were ready to read it," I said, pulling the letter out of my pocket.

Her whole face changed, and I felt bad because I knew how much she missed Ms. Mary. She started reading the letter, and tears were pouring down her face. I placed my arms around her as she cried. I saw the shock come over her when she read the part about her having a sister. I then saw the look of determination as she wiped away her tears and held the picture of her sister to her chest.

"I'm sorry that I kept it away from you this long, but I needed to make sure that you could handle yourself. Ms. Mary would be upset if I took you there without being prepared. That's another reason for all of the training that we have been doing. Now, I spoke with Zontae, and he said that we can take a hiatus from our security duties and go on this mission to find your sister. We can leave in the morning if you want to," I explained.

Lawrynn wiped her face and nodded 'yes' and replied, "Okay. I just want to find my sister. She is the only family in the world that I have. I just can't believe that Ms. Mary kept it from me. I will definitely be ready in the morning."

That went better than I thought.

Pop!

I felt a fist go across my face and tasted blood. Then there was a knee to my nuts that had me on the ground.

"That was for keeping the letter from me! I will be ready in the morning. Goodnight, Monroe," Lawrynn said as she stepped over me and left.

After my balls dropped back down into my nut sack, I stood up and limped to my room. Yep, that definitely went the way I thought it would.

MESA

*L*ife was lovely for me. I adjusted my crown as I was leaving from checking on Lene. I went into the nursery and kissed all the babies. Mena and Mesa Jr. were finally asleep as well as my niece and nephew. I knew that Lene was pregnant because her pussy felt different, and her ass was an emotional mess. I was hoping for a little girl to name after my grandmother, Mary.

Although we didn't know her well, she had sacrificed herself to stop my mother from wrecking any more havoc than she already had done. The realms were in chaos, and some things were jumping off in the human world also. This meeting was about putting together the pieces that Esha had left broken.

Our pops had stepped down completely and was devoting his time to taking care of Nichelle full-time. Santonio and he were bumping heads so much that I knew that any day they would come to blows. Something was going on with him too, I just couldn't put my finger on it. Whatever Esha and Luke did to him was messing with his mind. I told him he needed to start seeing Ever, and I was surprised he was listening and was attending sessions. Problem was, Ever would leave the sessions and look spooked. I needed to have a chat with her about that too. Fuck confidentiality! If something threatened my family, it needed to be handled.

I ran into Zoom right before I was about to head into the meeting room, and he looked troubled.

"What's going on with you, man? You look like you have the weight of the world on your shoulders," I asked him.

Zoom shook his head and sighed, "My father is up for parole. I haven't told Ever anything about him or why he is locked up in the state mental prison. I don't want her to think that I could end up like him too. My magic is becoming more powerful ever since I used it against the Seraphim. You know how I feel about magic, and now I am having to release it just to ease the pressure. Not to mention, Syren has been moping around our house, because Alpha and Omega are pissed off about her being mated to Vice also. They come over to feed her, but they won't speak to her."

I shook my head because my cousins were being petty. There was no way in hell that I would let another man claim my mate as his own. She would be in my bed getting fucked until she had no memory of that motherfucker, but that was just me I guess. I needed to have a talk with both of them, because Duvall men didn't let another man rule where his dick rested.

"I will have a chat with Omega and Alpha and see if I can't get them to have a chat with their mate. As far as your father, Ever is a head doctor. She should understand what's going on. Hell, she might be able to help him and you out. Magic is a part of you, Zoom, and you can't keep ignoring it or pushing it down inside of you. Talk to your mate, man, and if you want help with controlling your magic, you need to talk to Dane. I don't like his ass, but since Nichelle is out of commission, you need to speak to him about it. You know we got you in whatever, man," I stated and gave him a side hug.

"Thanks, bruh. I hear everything that you said, and I am going to figure out what's going on with me. I will talk to Ever and tell her what's going on. I know she has the time to see me since Christy headed back to college," Zoom stated.

We headed in, and I took a breath to prepare myself for the shit that was to come for this meeting. I had somewhat fixed Zoom's problems, now it was Zontae's turn to fix the world's. I didn't envy my brother one bit.

KING ZONTAE

*E*veryone was gathered in the meeting room, and the voices were overwhelming as they argued about whose realm had the most problems. The saying be careful what you wish for came to mind. I picked up the gavel and pounded it on the table.

"Alright, let's get down to business. I need for everyone to follow the rules and not to talk until it's your turn. Now that the coronation is finished, I have some announcements to make. First of all, there will be no more council. Each and every king will have a vote at the table. If there is a tie, then I as the King of the Underworld will cast the final vote. King Bayou, report that status of your realm," I ordered.

"My people are dying in the ocean. Esha must have polluted the waters with some type of chemical, because our fins and scales are breaking out in spots or just falling off completely. I am not sure of what to do right now. I heard there is a marine biologist that could possibly help. I am searching for her, and I will see if she can solve the mystery," King Bayou stated.

I nodded and replied, "Find the marine biologist and see if she can help. In the meantime, have your people swim in the rivers and the lakes. It's not the oceans, but it should be safe for now."

The day continued with me listening to all of the kings and their troubles in their realms. Things were bad in the human world with something attacking humans and ripping their throats out. Ro and Ace were helping us out on finding out what they were. They had killed the creatures that Esha had in the basement, but we thought that she had more of them stashed somewhere else. Slice had officially taken over the B-pack business and the Dynasty Boyz. Cas had hit one of our major houses and stole our supply. Slice was the one that would have to deal with her and get our shit back. I could go on and on with the chaos that Esha had caused.

The thing that I had learned was, no matter what, being king was hell. The only things that made it all worth it was my family and friends. We had been through hell and back, but we were still here. I was not a perfect king, but I was the best one that I could be. In the words of the people that depended on me, 'May the Most High bless King Zontae's Reign.'

JADE

MEANWHILE IN MEXICO...

$\mathcal{I}$ sat shaking, waiting on them to perform the ritual. They were sprinkling holy water all around, and they were wielding crucifixes as they circled around. After two hours, the nun came to me. She had tears in her eyes and was carrying a bundle wrapped in blankets.

"We tried everything we could, but he still has it inside of him. I am sorry, and we will be praying for you," she said as she handed over the bundle and ran off.

I cried as I pulled the blankets back and stared into my son's jet-black eyes. He stared at me with such hate and disappointment. It would be that way every time I brought him to church or the convent. I left him on the steps of different orphanages, but the next morning, he would be right back in his crib. I was stuck with a monster, and there was nothing to do about it. Fuck my life. Karma was a bitch!

The End-
Keep reading if you want more Underworld...

WORD FROM THE AUTHOR...

Thank you so much for reading and loving *Underworld Zontae's Reign*. Many of you have asked me to continue with this paranormal series. Although Zontae's Reign is ending, I am happy to announce that there will be a paranormal series spin-off called *Kings of the Underworld*.

They will tell the stories of Alpha, Omega, Slice, Monroe, Kaidan, Bayou, and Zoom. The first one will be *Kings of the Underworld: The Demon Realm* featuring Alpha and Omega, coming late summer. I hope you enjoyed it!

Please leave a review and let me know what you thought. Thank you!

A NOTE FROM THE AUTHOR

Thank you for taking the time to read my work.
Follow me on my social media to find out about upcoming projects
and work.

Website: www.annitialjackson.com
Facebook:https://www.facebook.com/DCityChronicles/?
ref=aymt_homepage_panel#
Instagram: https://www.instagram.com/annitialjackson/
Twitter: https://twitter.com/ANNITIALJACKSON

THE TRINITY GIRL CHRONICLES: THE GOLDEN CROWN"

Lia, Tootie, and Jame` have been training for months, learning their new powers and preparing to battle the Chaos Squad. They are thrown for a loop when the Chaos Squad decides to bring the battle to them by enrolling in their school.

The Chaos Squad is on the hunt for the missing golden crown that could free their father for good. The problem is, the boys are starting to not trust each other, and that could put their plans in jeopardy.

Can the Chaos squad get it together and find the crown? Or will the Trinity Girls succeed in finding it first?

ABOUT THE AUTHOR

This is book nine for me, and I'm excited to be able to share my work and creativity with all my old and new readers. As a new author in this literary world, I'm encouraged by your reviews and your willingness to read and hopefully enjoy my work. If you would like to join my reading group, I am on Facebook, and the name of the group is Bossy Book Babes.

To my publisher, Quiana, I am thankful for the opportunity and humbled that you allow me to use my pen to display my craft. You are an inspiration, and I thank you for allowing me to create books using my crazy imagination. Thank you for your guidance and motivation that you instill in me. To my pen sisters and brothers, thank you for your undying love and support as I navigate as one of the newest members of the Major Key family. Thank you to the editing staff for making sure that my work shines!

To my readers... words cannot express what you mean to me. Thank you for reading my work and giving me critiques to help me better my craft. I am always available to hear your comments and opinions. I love you, ALJ readers!

ALSO BY ANNITIA L. JACKSON

Please check out my other titles listed on Amazon and Barnes & Noble:

D-City Chronicles Book One: Aja and Ro

D-CITY Chronicles Book Two: Aja and Ro

D-City Chronicles: The Finale

The Trinity Girl Chronicles: The Awakening

An Urban Christmas Story: Ebb and Bobbi

D-City Underworld: Zontae's Reign

D-City Underworld 2: Zontae's Reign

Loving a Heartless Queen